A DEN OF TRICKS

A SHADE OF VAMPIRE 54

BELLA FORREST

ALSO BY BELLA FORREST

HOTBLOODS

(Brand new paranormal romance series!)

Hotbloods (Book 1)

Coldbloods (Book 2)

Renegades (Book 3)

THE GIRL WHO DARED TO THINK

The Girl Who Dared to Think (Book 1)

The Girl Who Dared to Stand (Book 2)

The Girl Who Dared to Descend (Book 3)

The Girl Who Dared to Rise (Book 4)

The Girl Who Dared to Lead (Book 5)

THE GENDER GAME

(Completed series)

The Gender Game (Book 1)

The Gender Secret (Book 2)

The Gender Lie (Book 3)

The Gender War (Book 4)

The Gender Fall (Book 5)

The Gender Plan (Book 6)

The Gender End (Book 7)

A SHADE OF VAMPIRE SERIES

Series 1: Derek & Sofia's story

A Shade of Vampire (Book 1)

A Shade of Blood (Book 2)

A Castle of Sand (Book 3)

A Shadow of Light (Book 4)

A Blaze of Sun (Book 5)

A Gate of Night (Book 6)

A Break of Day (Book 7)

Series 2: Rose & Caleb's story

A Shade of Novak (Book 8)

A Bond of Blood (Book 9)

A Spell of Time (Book 10)

A Chase of Prey (Book 11)

A Shade of Doubt (Book 12)

A Turn of Tides (Book 13)

A Dawn of Strength (Book 14)

A Fall of Secrets (Book 15)

An End of Night (Book 16)

Series 3: The Shade continues with a new hero...

A Wind of Change (Book 17)

A Trail of Echoes (Book 18)

A Soldier of Shadows (Book 19)

A Hero of Realms (Book 20)

A Vial of Life (Book 21)

A Fork of Paths (Book 22)

A Flight of Souls (Book 23)

A Bridge of Stars (Book 24)

Series 4: A Clan of Novaks

A Clan of Novaks (Book 25)

A World of New (Book 26)

A Web of Lies (Book 27)

A Touch of Truth (Book 28)

An Hour of Need (Book 29)

A Game of Risk (Book 30)

A Twist of Fates (Book 31)

A Day of Glory (Book 32)

Series 5: A Dawn of Guardians

A Dawn of Guardians (Book 33)

A Sword of Chance (Book 34)

A Race of Trials (Book 35)

A King of Shadow (Book 36)

An Empire of Stones (Book 37)

A Power of Old (Book 38)

A Rip of Realms (Book 39)

A Shade of Kiev 2

A Shade of Kiev 3

THE SECRET OF SPELLSHADOW MANOR

(Completed series)

The Secret of Spellshadow Manor (Book 1)

The Breaker (Book 2)

The Chain (Book 3)

The Keep (Book 4)

The Test (Book 5)

The Spell (Book 6)

BEAUTIFUL MONSTER DUOLOGY

Beautiful Monster 1

Beautiful Monster 2

DETECTIVE ERIN BOND (Adult thriller/mystery)

Lights, Camera, GONE

Write, Edit, KILL

For an updated list of Bella's books, please visit her website: www.bellaforrest.net

Join Bella's VIP email list and she'll send you an email reminder as soon as her next book is out. Visit to sign up: www.forrestbooks.com

NEW GENERATION LIST

- **Avril (vampire):** adopted daughter of Lucas and biological daughter of Marion.
- **Blaze (fire dragon):** son of fire dragons Heath and Athena.
- **Caia (part fae/human):** daughter of Grace and Lawrence.
- **Fiona (vampire):** daughter of Benedict (son of Rose and Caleb) and Yelena.
- **Harper (sentry/vampire):** daughter of Hazel and Tejus.
- **Scarlett (vampire):** daughter of Jeramiah (son of Lucas Novak) and Pippa (daughter of Cameron Hendry).

FAMILY TREE

If you'd like to check out the Novaks' family tree, visit: **www.forrestbooks.com/tree**

1

HARPER

(DAUGHTER OF HAZEL & TEJUS)

It didn't take long for the Correction Officers to clear out the top level of Azure Heights, in the wake of the horrendous attack on the Five Lords' mansions. There were many questions left unanswered, but the few things we knew were enough to get us through the night and one step closer to cracking the mystery surrounding the Exiled Maras' tormented existence on Neraka.

Darius of House Xunn was dead. That was a fact. His daughter, Rewa, was in Vincent's care at the White Star Hotel on the level below. Dozens of Imen and Maras from all five Houses had been killed in the two explosions that tore into the Lords' mansions. The main blast came from House Xunn. The second detonation took place shortly afterward, but we weren't sure of its origin. The daemons were the most likely culprits. They were far better organized than we'd initially given them credit for, and they were in possession of powerful swamp witch magic. They roamed through the Valley of Screams, and they consumed souls.

That was all that we knew for sure, along with the fact that the interplanetary travel spell no longer worked, as evidenced by Avril's attempt and near-death experience less than an hour earlier. We had no way of reaching out to Calliope, and our only hope rested in GASP sending reinforcements, since they'd most likely realized that Telluris wasn't working, either. The sooner, the better, based on what was going on here.

They should've been here by now...

My biggest fear was that anyone trying to cross the asteroid belt into Neraka would experience the same as Avril when we tried to send her *out*. We must have all been thinking it, but none of us had the courage to voice it. We had enough on our plates as it was.

Everything else weighed heavy with question marks. Even the trust we'd put into the Exiled Maras was left on shaky ground, mainly because they were the only possible connection that the daemons could've had to swamp witch magic.

I glanced around, watching as Correction Officers carried the last bodies away—they were all going to the fourth floor, where the funeral home servants awaited, to begin preparations for the next day. There was going to be a mass burial, and we were going to add Minah's body to it, too.

Patrik, Caia, Blaze, and Fiona were downstairs in the infirmary, preparing for their missions. Patrik had charm satchels to prepare, which Blaze and Caia would take into the underground prison and place in the north, south, west, and east walls, expanding the Druid's original protection spell. They were also going to repaint the red symbols here on the top floor, given that everything I'd painted before had come down with the walls. They could easily repaint them on four trees facing each direction around the mansion. Fiona was going to use the invisibility spell and sneak into the prison with Blaze and Caia. Her task was to find and rescue Demios—we hoped that, once we freed him, Arrah would be more willing to speak up about the Exiled Maras. There were things they weren't telling us, information that Arrah wouldn't disclose with her brother in prison.

Jax, Hansa, Scarlett, Avril, Heron, and I stayed on the top level with the remaining Lords. We had plenty to talk about—though I had a feeling they wouldn't be easy to talk to. They were all dazed and grieving.

"How did the daemons get their claws on swamp witch magic?" Jax was the first to speak up after the level was cleared and Correction Officers were stationed at the bottom of the staircase, to keep everyone away.

The Lords didn't seem all that surprised by the question, but they looked genuinely baffled as they slowly shook their heads.

"I don't know," Emilian replied. "Vincent told us about your discoveries in the Valley of Screams, but... but it doesn't make any sense."

"You're going to have to give us more to go on here, because right now you look like the source of swamp witch magic for the daemons. And that makes no damn sense, since they're the ones hunting and killing you off, one by one," Jax said, crossing his arms over his chest.

"You don't understand." Emilian raised his arms in a defensive gesture. "We don't know. The swamp witch from that Druid delegation never gave us an invisibility spell. The only potent magic we have is the interplanetary spell! Everything else—and by that, I mean literally five small spells—is just charms we use to support the growth of our crops and animals... to preserve our blood resources and to generally make our lives easier."

We stared at each other for a long moment, as Avril used her sharp sense of smell to notice changes in the Lords' behavior. I could tell, from the way her nostrils flared and her head moved, that she was trying to pick up on the subtle chemical fluctuations that might signal deception. Judging by the faint frown on her face, there wasn't anything of use.

"That's not a good answer, I'll be honest." Hansa sighed. "Because that leaves us with a very unpleasant question still hanging over our heads: who gave swamp witch magic to the daemons?"

"It's not something you simply come across," Jax added. "Could there have been a *second* delegation to Neraka, before your people were exiled here, perhaps? And the daemons got a hold of it, somehow?"

"There's no way of knowing for sure." Farrah shrugged,

wiping the soot from her face with a silken handkerchief she kept in her dress pocket.

"What are the odds?" Emilian shook his head. "I... I don't know. I'm honestly baffled. And terrified, because that means the daemons are far more powerful than we thought. Although, to be fair, we know a lot more about our enemy today than we did four nights ago, thanks to you."

He gave us an appreciative nod—a gesture we all briefly returned.

"They targeted Darius, but used enough explosive to kill as many of us as possible," Emilian continued, gazing at the remains of House Xunn. Sadness drew his eyebrows into a frown. "They must have known about the dinner party at his place. Maybe they were looking to send us a message after your performance in the Valley of Screams."

"Retaliation, you mean," I replied, while mentally going over the events. The timeline didn't exactly work, since this had all happened in the same day. "They would've needed time to plan. To come here and plant the explosive, not long after we returned. They would've had to know about the dinner party, too, if they were going for maximum casualties. I'm not sure that works..."

"What if they didn't know? What if they just wanted to strike us hard and fast, and Darius's house was the most convenient target?" Jax offered an opposing argument that actually made more sense.

"That would be swift retribution," Rowan said, gazing out

into the distance, where the gorges rose over the plain, black giants beneath the night sky through which the three moons traveled lazily. "Either way, this was meant to send us a message. To break us down."

"Like that will ever happen," Farrah scoffed, then glanced over her shoulder, a pained expression turning the corners of her mouth downward as she analyzed from afar what was left of her mansion.

"We cannot let them divide us," Emilian concluded. "We cannot let them keep hurting us and taking our loved ones. They've become far too brazen. This must stop."

"We should keep our Correction Officers focused on the city's protection," Caspian interjected. "I'm not comfortable with sending them out to fight these fiends, not when there aren't that many of us to begin with."

"I hate it!" Farrah grumbled. "It makes me feel so powerless, when all I want to do is go out there and show them what we're made of!"

"Lord Kifo has a point. And we're doing our best here, too," Jax replied, "but until more GASP teams arrive, there isn't much we can do in terms of retaliation, since we don't know exactly how many daemons there are. But what we can do is increase the protections on the city and make sure that these horned monsters don't get away with so many murders. We've already taken many of them down. We'll keep doing it until Calliope sends us backup."

Jax was right. We didn't have enough supernatural power to

tackle an entire nation of these fiends. I mean, sure, we had one dragon, but that didn't suffice before thousands of daemons. We needed the rest of Blaze's clan. Hell, we could use some ice dragons, too. More Druids, and some witches. Perhaps even Viola, if the Daughters of Eritopia found themselves willing to lend Neraka a hand.

But we didn't have them, for the time being. We only had ourselves, and a city full of innocent people to protect.

2

AVRIL

(DAUGHTER OF LUCAS & MARION)

I left the conversation to sniff out any clues around the remains of the mansions, as the Lords and Jax were already moving on to logistical details that I could be briefed on later. To me it was more important to uncover any evidence that could be traced back to the culprits behind this attack, and the rest of my team agreed.

The houses had been mostly torn down, with fragments of walls and support pillars still standing here and there. The bodies had all been recovered, and I was left with a large number of piles consisting mostly of burnt wood, ashes, and rubble. My olfactory sense was bombarded with a base note of death and charred flesh, something akin to a barbecue gone wrong, and it broke my heart.

Nevertheless, I had to focus. Closing my eyes as I stood in the middle of what had, until earlier, been the residence of House Xunn, I homed in on the other, more elusive scents. Heron was somewhere nearby, looking through the rubble near the center of the first explosion for anything that could help us understand what kind of explosives were used.

I caught a whiff of something sharp and heavy, and it scratched at the back of my throat like charcoal powder. It was different from everything else I'd identified so far as common household items, including soaps and cooking oils. I followed the trail and found myself standing in front of Heron. He pulled out a thin stick of what looked like melted plastic.

He noticed my gaze fixated on the object in question, and handed it over. I brought it up to my nose and took a deep breath.

"This is it," I murmured, then coughed as the smell invaded my airways like sticky dust. It reminded me of gunpowder, but it seemed more potent and intense. It was a foreign chemical, and I had no way of ascertaining what it was, exactly, but there was one thing I could do while Heron continued to dig through the pile. "Do you have a lighter?"

Heron gave me one of the two he always kept with him—it was team policy to always carry a source of fire for Caia to have handy, in case she ever lost hers. Mine had been destroyed during my attempt to leave the planet. I flicked it open and produced a small flame, then placed the flame against one end of the melted stick.

It burst like a raging firework. I yelped and dropped it, especially alarmed because I was still reeling from the earlier interplanetary spell disaster that had nearly claimed my life. My body had already healed, but my inner wounds were still fresh. Both Heron and I stared at the stick as the fire ate away at it—it popped and hissed as sparks flew out.

I glanced to my left, where the Lords and the rest of my team were standing, and noticed the frowns on the Exiled Maras' faces.

"That's *ephelis*," Caspian said, his eyes on the rapidly burning stick at my feet. "It's a powder we make from certain mineral deposits in the caves around the mountain. It's highly flammable. Our craftsmen blend it into a paste and make those sticks out of it. We use them to blow up sections of stone... It's how we built the levels of Mount Azure."

"So it's a local explosive," I concluded.

"Yes, and that's a major problem because we only have one workshop that manufactures these things, and its ephelis reserve is meant to be under lock and key," he replied, then snapped his fingers at one of the Correction Officers waiting at the bottom of the stairs. The uniformed Mara came up, and gave Caspian a brief nod. "Go check in on Master Dresdel. The explosives came from his workshop."

The Correction Officer obeyed and rushed downstairs to one of the lower levels of the city. Heron and I started digging through the rubble and cleared out another handful of melted sticks.

"These didn't ignite all the way, I'm guessing," I said, looking at Caspian while pointing down at our finding. His nod confirmed my suspicion. I shifted my focus back to the rubble at our feet. "This was very sloppily put together, then. Had the detonator been more accurate, these would've substantially amplified the explosion."

Heron found the tip of a slim black tube, and tugged it until it revealed a small piece of what must have been a mechanical device. There was another tube attached to it, but it led nowhere, as the other end had been torn in the explosion, and the flames must have burned through the rest.

"This must have been a part of the detonator," Heron said slowly.

He then glanced around, his jade eyes looking for other traces of the tube. I gripped the burnt end of the detonator tube and sniffed it. There was something rubbery in it, with a faint note of sulfur. It was enough for me to start tracing its remains around the center of the explosion. Heron noticed me moving toward the back of the house, and quietly followed.

"Stop," he said, then bent down and retrieved a solitary piece of the same detonator tube. "Yeah, you're going the right way."

"Good. This has to lead somewhere. There's definitely a main mechanical detonator, a shock tube of sorts. Air pressure was used to ignite the one in the house. I'm sure it was detonated remotely, but it wasn't well made," I replied.

"Which means that whoever did this isn't exactly an expert

with explosives," Heron muttered, watching as I walked closer to what used to be the kitchen door leading out to the back garden.

"And that could also mean that they may not be experts at concealing their tracks, either." I nodded and picked up the scent of more burnt tubes.

Heron found another fragment, this one longer. The farther we got from the center of the blast, the better preserved our evidence was. Soon after that, we found a junction piece—two slim shock tubes, one of which came from House Xunn, tied up into a thicker one.

"Follow the main shock tube," I suggested to Heron, "and I'll follow this second one."

He nodded and scoured the back garden, its grass and flowers burnt down, embers still glowing in the fractured remains of the wooden gazebo. This had once been a corner of comfort and peace, and it made my stomach churn to see it like this.

I traced the second tube to House Kifo. There was another detonator buried under the pile of wood and stone that had once been the kitchen. I pulled it out of the rubble as Caspian stared at me and the object, apparently in a stupor.

"You mean to tell me the second explosion came from *my* house?" he said, almost out of breath. Harper stood next to him, her eyes wide with shock, her brow settling into a concerned frown.

"It appears so." I shrugged, sniffing the melted device, then looking down. "But this was also poorly put together. There are several intact sticks of ephelis at the bottom. I can see them from here."

"Found the main detonator." Heron came out of the woods behind the tattered stables facing House Xunn, holding another, larger mechanical device in his hands. The main shock tube was still attached to it, and it covered several yards in length. It had been built with a pump, from what I could tell at first glance. "It was twenty yards behind the stables, at the base of a tree."

"Remote detonation." I nodded slowly. "Just as I thought. This was planned, but it required knowledge of both the Xunn and Kifo households to plant the explosives. If this was retaliation for what we did in the gorges, then their timing was way too good."

"True." Heron came by my side, and we both looked at the Lords and the rest of our team. "They only had what, three, four hours since we left the Valley of Screams?"

They all mulled over the information for a while. Heron and I continued to look through the rubble of the Kifo mansion for anything else that could be of use. We then moved our search into the woods, where Heron had found the main detonator.

"Maybe I can pick up a scent here," I said as we walked over to the tree in question.

"Avril, I... I need to talk to you." Heron caught my right forearm before I could circle the tree for foreign scents. I gazed up at him with both eyebrows raised.

"What is it?" I asked, trying to hold it together. His touch triggered tiny electrical currents flowing through my arms. My heart started pounding, a sensation I was still getting accustomed to whenever he was near me.

He needed a few moments to put his thoughts in order, judging by the way his eyes absently darted around me before they settled on my face.

"I... I need you to be more careful from now on," he replied, his eyebrows drawn closer, his gaze clouded.

"What do you mean?" I shrugged. "We already know what happened here. No one's coming at us at this point. It would be foolish."

"I'm not talking about this. I'm talking about you. Just... Please, be more careful. No more volunteering for swamp witch travel spells and stuff like that. It's just... Just don't."

"Neither of us knew what was going to happen up there, Heron. It's not like I had any plans to get myself burned alive." I sighed.

"I know, but... but I almost lost you back there." The pained look on his face floored me, and I had to swallow back the bundle of emotions working its way up my throat for some reason. "I have never experienced something like that, Avril, and I don't want to feel it ever again."

"What... What are you talking about?" My brain slowed down, leaving my body in charge as he gently pulled me closer to him.

"I like having you around," he replied, his expression softening a little as the shadow of a smile passed over his lips. "So, you know, just be careful."

I needed a minute to take it all in. Was this Heron's way of telling me that he liked me? That he was into me? ...Maybe as much as I was into him?

"Okay, I promise to do my best not to get myself blown up again." I gave him a wink, trying to diffuse some of the tension I felt building up. The longer we gazed at each other, the thicker the air between us grew.

He licked his lower lip, then bit it. He let go of my arm, put his hands behind his back, and looked away, somewhere to his left. A muscle twitched in his jaw, and I had a feeling he had more to say, so I waited patiently. I continued asking myself the same questions in the back of my head—what was he really telling me with "I like having you around"?

"You know, I've never done Pyrope before, with anyone," he breathed, then shifted his focus back to me. "It's a very important ritual to me. I was hoping I'd share my first Pyrope with my soulmate one day."

It hit me then what he was talking about. I'd offered him my blood back in the Valley of Screams, of my own accord. He'd taken that as Pyrope, the Mara ritual in which non-Maras give their blood willingly, either as a one-off or as a recurring experience. The only solid example I was aware of was the deal between Jax and Zeriel, King of the Tritones. But I also knew that Pyrope was often practiced by mixed couples, and it was a very intimate thing to do.

"I... I'm sorry," I mumbled, lowering my head and suddenly feeling out of place. "I guess I ruined Pyrope for you, but you know we had no choice. I mean, you were injured, and we needed you healed fast, given our circumstances."

His fingers gripped my chin as he lifted my head. His gaze found my eyes again, and he gave me a soft smile that sent waves of sunshine through my body, rippling toward the tips of my fingers and toes. He'd never looked at me like that.

"Don't be sorry," he replied. "I just didn't expect my first Pyrope to happen so... fast and unexpected, so broken from tradition, that's all. I'm not unsatisfied by it happening."

I stilled. Was I hearing him right? He'd just mentioned experiencing his first Pyrope with his soulmate, but that the circumstances were different from what he'd imagined. Was this his veiled way of telling me that I meant more to him, or was this just me misinterpreting his words?

"Wait... what do you mean, Heron?" I asked, feeling my heart thudding in my chest.

"I guess I—"

"Heron, Avril, come over here for a minute," Hansa called out, interrupting him.

Argh... Horrible timing!

Heron gave me an apologetic look, and I gave him a brief nod in return, hoping we'd get to resume this conversation later. I took a deep breath and followed him back to the group on the edge of the first level.

My only fear was that I'd misunderstood what he'd just said.

It scared me more than I'd thought it could, probably because I was genuinely falling for Heron and I dreaded the thought of it all being one-sided.

3

JAX

There were too many things going through my head at once, on top of what had already happened before the explosions. I was having a hard time holding it all together, so I tried prioritizing first, and did my best to focus on the attack on the Lords' mansions.

I could easily blame Hansa for throwing me off balance like that. The impact of her kiss was far more devastating than I'd originally thought. My blood was constantly simmering and my senses were amplified in her presence, as if every atom in my body were suddenly energized just from being close to her.

The worst part was the mixture of pain and shame I felt on the inside, where she was concerned. I'd fallen in love with her, so hard and fast, from our first encounters back on Calliope. After her near-death experience at the hands of Azazel, however, I'd shoved those feelings somewhere deep down, where it was meant to be dark and cold enough for them to never resurface.

Yet all it took was for me to see her every day for my heart to thaw. Feeling her lips on mine was the ignition point of no return, but all I managed to do was hurt her again. I was terrified of falling for her because of my tragic past experiences, and I hadn't even thought of what my wavering did to her.

I'd have to make it up to her. There was no point in denying it anymore. I loved her. It was just a matter of getting myself settled into that mindset, and gaining some form of control over the situation. We were in a strange and hostile territory, and the last thing I wanted was to go back to Calliope with her remains. I needed to focus on her safety, so we could both go back and take this... this thing between us to the next level.

Until then, however, I had to come forward as the leader she expected me to be. She'd challenged me, and I was determined to prove to her that I was the Mara she'd met back home. The best way for me to do this was to find a way to take the fight back into the Valley of Screams.

Provided that the Druid could amplify and expand the protection spell over the city, we could focus on retaliation. The daemons had struck back hard, but we weren't done yet. On top of that, Avril's discovery had shed light on how fast the fiends operated, and what their shortcomings were.

"What's up?" Avril asked as she and Heron rejoined the conversation. My brother had a peculiar look on his face, but that was a conversation best saved for later.

"We've been talking about the daemons' way of operating," I replied, "and I think it's time we organize another incursion into the gorges."

"What for?" Heron frowned, stealing a glance at Avril.

I knew it!

My little brother had the hots for the young vampire, which meant there was still hope for him to recover from his imprisonment trauma. I'd feared I'd be left to deal with his philandering nonsense for an eternity.

"Well, think about it this way," I said. "The daemons were able to put together a counterattack in a matter of hours, and they clearly had knowledge of the mansions' layouts and the Lords' movements. This means they're highly organized, despite their sloppy but still devastating explosive charges. I don't think we can just stay here and wait for GASP to come for us. Every day that we spend here counts. We should go back into the Valley of Screams and look for a way into their underground cities. Scope out the enemy... find out what else they're hiding down there, besides swamp witch spells, armored daemons, and pit wolves."

The Lords glanced at each other, then looked at me and nodded vehemently.

"We'll arrange for Correction Officers to join you again," Emilian replied with determination. "How many would you need?"

"None," I replied, prompting my team to raise a collective eyebrow at me.

"What do you mean by 'none'?" Hansa asked.

"If we're going in there for recon, we can't have a large group to draw attention," I explained. "Just a handful of us, with enough invisibility paste handy in case we need it. We need to be swift and quiet, make good use of shadows and blind spots."

Heron then gave me a conspiratorial grin as he patted my shoulder.

"I get it!" he replied. "We go in, a handful of us, capture ourselves a hunter daemon or two, and force them to take us down below. Right?"

"Exactly." I nodded. "And since they'll be carrying their own, modified version of the invisibility spell, we can use it to replenish our resources, since we'll be infiltrating enemy territory."

I noticed the expressions on my team's faces change from uncertain to somewhat enlightened, as they understood the premise of a scouting mission. Harper took a step forward, her hands resting on her sword handles.

"Okay, I'm in," she said. "How do we do this?"

Her energy was very much welcomed. We were all tired after the night and day we'd spent in the Valley of Screams, first looking for Fiona, then making our way back into the city. We'd failed with the interplanetary spell and were clearly stuck on Neraka, for the time being. And the daemons had just carried out a deadly attack on the Five Lords—who were now Four.

I glanced at Hansa, and I knew, deep down, that she was coming with me, whether I liked it or not. She wasn't going to take no for an answer, no matter how much I needed her here, in the city, in relative safety as opposed to in the gorges.

It was definitely one of the reasons I'd fallen for her in the first place. She was fearless.

And she stood by my side, even when I faltered and foolishly rejected her.

4

HARPER

(DAUGHTER OF HAZEL & TEJUS)

"I know I'm going," Jax said, then nodded to Hansa, "and I know she's going."

"And I've already called dibs on the third spot on this mission." I smirked, eager to get deeper into enemy territory and learn everything I could before we could deliver a large-scale, devastating blow and wipe those horned bastards off the face of Neraka.

"And we'll take Caia and Blaze with us again," Jax replied, looking at Heron, Avril, Patrik and Scarlett. "We'll need that firepower down there, in case something goes wrong. You four stay here with the rest of the team. The city needs GASP in the aftermath of what just happened."

The Lords watched quietly as Jax laid out the plan. Caspian was next to me, and I could feel his gaze on the side of my face. I gave him a brief glance and felt my heart skip a beat. There was a peculiar warmth in his jade eyes, the kind of emotion that promised sweet, beautiful moments, in a dramatic contrast with what had been happening in Azure Heights.

"What do you need us to do here?" Avril asked.

"You and Heron can start questioning witnesses regarding the explosions," Jax said. "Use a broader timeline, though. From this morning until right now. Someone must have seen something out of place. Start with the Imen and Maras who were on this level."

He then glanced up at the asteroid belt, a string of shimmering purplish dots in the sky, and frowned, then shifted his focus to Fiona.

"You can assist Patrik and Scarlett with their research," he said to her. "We need to find out what's happening with that asteroid belt, too. GASP may already be on their way here, but we'll still have to get off Neraka at some point, preferably in the near future. We can't do that if the asteroids continue to jam our magic."

Fiona nodded firmly, and Scarlett put her arm around her shoulders. Despite everything that had just happened, I could still breathe easier with Fiona back from the Valley of Screams. As long as our team was intact and strong, we stood a better chance against the daemons.

"I'd like to join you on this mission, if you'll have me," Caspian interjected, giving me a brief sideways glance.

Jax and Hansa looked at each other for a moment; then they both nodded.

"It would be an honor to have you with us," Jax replied. "Provided the other Lords will not suffer any setbacks in your absence. We wouldn't want to disrupt your activities in any way, especially after what just happened."

"That won't be an issue," Caspian said, just as Emilian opened his mouth to reply. "I'll leave Cadmus in charge while I'm away. I feel like you need one of us with you on this journey, and, given the recent development, I feel like we need to address this trust issue between GASP and the Exiled Maras."

Emilian, Farrah, and Rowan exchanged glances, as if they didn't even need words to communicate. Emilian then placed a hand on Caspian's shoulder, squeezing firmly.

"The Lords trust your judgment, as always, Caspian," he said, his voice soft but his gaze cold, unyielding, as if there were more beneath his words—something that Caspian needed to be aware of. It triggered a little question mark in my head, but I knew this wasn't the time to ask. Caspian owed me an answer, anyway. I'd have to slip that in. "Besides, Cadmus is more than capable of acting as your emissary."

I knew Jax and Hansa were more than eager to have Caspian with us. Lord Kifo was the only Exiled Mara they trusted—he'd more than proven his noble intentions, despite the many questions he'd left unanswered.

Caspian could even help us find a way into the underground city of daemons, but that was a conversation best left for later, maybe in one of his meranium chambers—provided I'd be able to get him into one. Either way, his offer to join us worked for me, too. There was so much about him that I didn't know, and something had definitely changed between us, from the moment I'd given him my blood to drink.

There was a glimmer in his eyes that I hadn't noticed before. Whenever he looked at me, something lit up beneath his dark eyelashes, and I couldn't help but hold my breath for a split second. It was as if he could see right into my soul. And I didn't mind it one bit.

On the contrary, I delighted in his attention, mostly because it amplified the emotions coming out of him—waves of gold, red, and murky green that I was doing my best to interpret accurately. Mom had once told me that it takes a while to attune oneself to someone's soul, as a sentry—the more time we spent together, the better I'd be able to read him.

"We should go back to the infirmary for now," Jax said, his gaze fixed on Emilian. "We'll see you in the morning, Lord Obara. What time will the funerals take place?"

Emilian sighed, the grief returning to his expression with a dark crease between his eyebrows. Both Farrah and Rowan leaned against him, and he put his arms around their shoulders. They were in this together, after all. I felt sorry for them, and I hoped we'd get our chance to pay the daemons in kind for what they had done to these people.

"We will begin the procession at nine," Emilian replied, a slight tremor in his voice confirming the suffering already visible on his face. "Rewa will be appointed Lady of Azure Heights, now that Darius is... gone."

"She is the eldest of House Xunn, and we need all five Houses to come through during these trying times." Rowan sighed.

"We'll leave you to talk among yourselves and to rest, then." Jax nodded slowly, then looked at Avril. "You and Heron stay behind and continue sifting through the remains. Look for anything that could be of any help. Come down to the infirmary afterward. We'll be there for another couple of hours, at least. We've got to go over the maps for tomorrow."

I figured that we could get a lot more done over a shorter period of time if there were more of us up here. My True Sight alone could significantly speed things along.

"I'd like to stay and help, if that's okay," I said. "I think I'm of more use up here, for now. You, Hansa, and Patrik could easily establish a route through the gorges for tomorrow..."

"Fair enough," Jax agreed, and gave Scarlett a gentle nudge. "Scarlett, you can stay too. You can all cover more ground together."

Emilian gave us a curt bow, then escorted Farrah and Rowan toward the stairs. He glanced over his shoulder, noticing Caspian still standing next to me.

"We're going to the White Star now. Rewa needs us to be there for her," Emilian said. "Will you join us, Caspian?"

"I'll come down later," Caspian replied softly. "I'm not very good at comforting the bereaved. I'm sure you know that. Perhaps I'll be of more use up here."

Emilian pursed his lips but didn't object. Instead, he went downstairs with Farrah and Rowan. Jax and Hansa left shortly afterward, leaving Avril, Heron, Scarlett, Caspian, and me to continue combing through the five mansions for any evidence we could use.

Of course, we were quite certain that the daemons were behind this. But the explosives used were local, and processed by an Exiled Mara craftsman. We couldn't draw any conclusions regarding that until Caspian's Correction Officer returned with the Mara in question.

Until then, however, there was still plenty of rubble to look through. With everything that had happened, my exhaustion was nowhere to be found.

We still had a lot to do. And I had a lot more to learn about Caspian. I was particularly intrigued by the shift in his attitude toward me. He'd been hot and cold—well, mostly cold—since the first day we'd met. I was dealing with a peculiarly warm Caspian now, and it made me feel all kinds of wonderfully strange.

5

HARPER

(DAUGHTER OF HAZEL & TEJUS)

An hour went by as we scoured the remains. Houses Xunn and Kifo remained central to our focus, as they'd been specifically targeted in this attack. Avril and Heron covered Darius's mansion, while Caspian and I looked through his, and Scarlett briefly scanned the other three.

Caspian's home was mostly destroyed, but there were parts of the first level still standing. After we checked the ground floor and found more traces of explosives, we moved upstairs. I used my True Sight to look through the piles of rubble, and found several notebooks in a metal box buried at the bottom.

I dug the box out as Caspian came to stand next to me. Its lock was melted shut, but I pried it open with my bare hands, and revealed its contents. I pulled one of the notebooks out, its pages soft and pale brown. This particular corner of the house had not been fully damaged, from what I could see. The note-book was a sketchbook, I realized as I flipped through it.

"Can I have that, please?" Caspian asked, his voice low and a flicker of sadness in his jade eyes. I nodded and handed it over. He looked through it, then looked at me. "I've been drawing since I was a little boy, especially after my parents died. It helped me handle the loneliness and loss."

I glanced at the pages and saw pencil portraits of his mother and father. Caspian would've been an accomplished artist if given the opportunity. His lines were firm and the contrasts were quite dramatic, but the overall compositions were beauti-ful. They showed a side of him I hadn't thought existed.

"You didn't want to forget their faces, did you?" I murmured.

"I already have," he sighed, "but I can always look at what I drew and the images come back, albeit a little hazy."

My chest tightened at the rawness in his voice. I could only imagine what it must've been like to grow up like he did, with nothing but a military regime instead of loving parents. His adoptive father must have been good to him, but I could tell from his demeanor that affection wasn't part of his daily life. Caspian had a hard time trusting people, and I was sure it stemmed from his childhood.

I flipped through another notebook and found sketches of daemons in different forms—from hunters to the armored ones we saw earlier, but others, too. Some were huge, with hunters hastily doodled on the side for scaling; others looked weak and covered in rags. I saw female daemons, too, with long hair and slim horns. Caspian had been drawing these for a while, from what I could tell. There were pit wolves and schematics of the gorge caves. He'd drawn other Exiled Maras, too, and panoramic views of the daemons' underground cities.

I looked up at him with questioning eyes, and he shrugged, a muscle twitching in his jaw.

"I promise I will tell you everything, Harper, as soon as I make sure that it won't put anyone's life at risk," he said gently, his gaze softening.

He was definitely different from the Caspian I'd known prior to the explosions. And the change felt more permanent. I didn't know what to do with that. My mind tumbled around the events since my first day on Neraka, as I tried to pick at the signs that might've pointed to this dynamic shift between us.

As far as I was concerned, it was getting harder to deny that I was developing feelings for him. I already felt closer to him simply because I could see his emotions. But I wasn't sure what those emotions were, as the colors changed back and forth and further confused me.

"I trust you will, at some point," I replied, then looked through another sketchbook, finding more drawings of daemons, one of which was massive and frightening enough to give *me* nightmares. "I'm sorry for your losses tonight, Lord Kifo. I'll do my best to punish those responsible."

A faint smile crossed his lips as he moved forward, leaving only a couple of inches between us. With him so close, I could see ribbons of gold emanating from him, like shimmering tendrils that warmed my face and chest. The jade pools in his eyes darkened, and he slowly lowered his head.

"Thank you for your blood tonight," he breathed. "Pyrope is a rare and beautiful gift for someone like me."

"It was the least I could do." I shrugged, the last part of his statement slipping past me for a second. "I mean, you healed me earlier, too, and I... Wait, Pyrope?"

My eyes widened as it all fell into place. He was right. I'd given him my blood, with my full consent. It wasn't exactly a pact, but still, the act of willfully giving him my blood could easily qualify as Pyrope. What had Jax told me about it? He did it with Zeriel, in return for his service, and Maras would sometimes engage in it with their non-Mara lovers.

Oh, dear...

Why was my mind rushing to the "non-Mara lovers" part, instead of the part regarding "services rendered"? Zeriel had paid with his blood when Jax saved his life.

Caspian gave me a soft smile, his lips inching closer to mine. Was that why he was suddenly so warm and gentle with me? Had my choice of giving him my blood changed the way he looked at me to such a dramatic extent?

"I mean... it's not technically Pyrope, is it?" I mumbled, as my heart performed a series of somersaults, kicking my stomach in the process.

"Not technically, but by a very loose definition," he replied, blinking slowly.

He seemed to look right into my soul, and the golden aura

around him seemed to intensify. My lips parted, mostly for me to breathe some air in, as I was getting a little lightheaded with him so close to me. His gaze dropped and his head moved an inch forward.

I froze, understanding right then and there that I *wanted* him to kiss me. Caspian Kifo, the mysterious and icy Exiled Mara I knew very little about. The seemingly ruthless leader who repeatedly saved me and even gave me his blood to heal me. The creature who had perfectly mastered the art of both drawing me in and pushing me away. I wanted him to kiss me.

But his lips never touched me.

Instead, his eyes found mine again as he took a deep breath, and the chills returned. He moved back and put the notebooks back in the metal box at my feet.

Caspian was flipping on me again. I could see dark green and red ribbons strangling the gold ones, his emotions shifting from what seemed like... affection, to something akin to distrust and pain, or anger. The red was particularly difficult to identify. My mom and dad never had trouble reading other people's feelings. Neither did Serena. They were able to interpret the colors with great precision, yet I was struggling with Caspian.

My inner sentry growled as he walked over to another corner, resuming the search. My shoulders dropped and I breathed out, slightly irritated—not so much by his hot and cold flips, but by my reaction to his close proximity. I was clearly into him, and that came with problems in a world like Neraka.

What were the chances something would even happen
between us?

Close to zero, maybe?

And why am I thinking about this? About him? Damn it, Harper,
snap out of it! You have a mission to focus on. People to save.
Come on!

One thing was still clear and impossible to refute at this
point: Caspian owed me a question. I was better off channeling
my energy into that. Asking the *right* question of the one creature on this planet who seemed to know more than everyone
else was crucial.

6

CAIA

(DAUGHTER OF GRACE & LAWRENCE)

Patrik prepared the charm satchels and red paint we needed to expand the protection spell into the underground and to redo the symbols that Harper had painted at the top level, along with the invisibility paste for Fiona.

I put them all in my backpack and checked my pockets for lighters. The chances of another daemon attack so soon after the explosions were minimal, but I couldn't risk it.

Patrik walked over to the dead daemon still lying on the table in the infirmary and muttered something under his breath. A soft golden light began to emanate from the creature's body as it was lifted a few inches above the table. He then took several rolls of bandages from a nearby cupboard and proceeded to wrap the daemon from head to toe.

"What are you doing, Patrik?" I asked, as Fiona swallowed the invisibility paste.

The Druid gave me a brief look before he resumed his work of carefully wrapping the creature.

"I'm preparing both bodies for their funeral," he replied. "Minah will join the procession tomorrow, but the daemon will need to be put to rest elsewhere. I'll most likely incinerate him in the morning before everyone else comes out."

"Why are you bothering yourself with giving the daemon a funeral service of *any* kind? He was a killer, a monster." Fiona frowned, slowly disappearing as the spell took effect.

"Because it's in my nature as a Druid." Patrik sighed, rolling the daemon's levitating body over as he unraveled a second bandage roll around his massive torso. This was a job for at least six rolls, judging by his size. "We honor life, no matter who it belongs to. Even the fiends back home—the Destroyers and the incubi that sided with Azazel and perished... We said a few words for them, too, when we burned their bodies outside Luceria. All life is precious, and all loss of life is tragic, regardless of how one's time in this world was spent. Besides, daemons are worthy opponents and ruthless warriors; they deserve a sliver of decency, unlike the Sluaghs back on Calliope..."

I nodded slowly. It kind of made sense, especially once I put myself in Patrik's shoes. He'd spent years as a Destroyer. He'd witnessed so many atrocities firsthand, reduced to being someone who inflicted pain, rather than fulfilling his Druid nature as a healer, a nurturer. He'd survived a war and decades of oppression, after all, and hadn't lost his common sense and decency. I glanced at the daemon and wondered if he had any family waiting for him. Who did he get himself killed for? A lover? A son? They all had a story, whether we wanted to acknowledge it or not.

"I don't know, Patrik," Blaze offered. "I think Rewa and the families of those who've lost loved ones to daemons might disagree..."

"Perhaps so." Patrik gave us a sad smile. "But it's in my nature to honor life and mourn death. It's more of a custom, rather than anything else. If I refrain from showing compassion even toward a daemon, then I am not faithful to Druid ethics and traditions. Even Azazel got a brief funeral. I burned his remains and spread them across the land. No one cried, of course, but nevertheless, his passing was observed."

"Thank you, Patrik, for not abandoning your nature. We're off now, and we'll see you in a bit," I said, and walked out.

Blaze and invisible Fiona followed, as one of Caspian's Correction Officers waited outside to take us into the prison.

"Here we go," Fiona whispered behind me.

"Good luck, Fi!" I breathed.

"Ready?" the Correction Officer asked as we reached him.

Blaze and I nodded, and he guided us up the stairs toward the third level and through a network of dark and narrow alleys, until we reached an old wall with a large iron door. The Mara pulled a lever back, causing it to screech loudly, and the door opened.

We went in, and walked through a corridor just as dark and narrow as the alleys for about fifty yards before a set of stairs took us all the way to the underground level in a tight spiral. I tried to keep my eyes on the lower part of the damp wall to my right—if I looked at the stairs, I could lose my balance.

Blaze was in front of me when Fiona slipped and bumped into me from behind, prompting a domino effect that ended with Blaze casually catching me in his arms. Fiona whispered an apology, and the Correction Officer gave us an over-the-shoulder frown.

"Sorry, I slipped!" I said out loud, for the Mara's ears, then looked up at Blaze, whose arms were still tightly wrapped around me, making my upper body tingle. "You can let go now…"

He inhaled deeply, then released me and continued descending the stairs. We quietly followed. Several minutes later, we reached the prison. The temperature had dropped by a couple degrees, further confirming that we were deep underground.

There was a large iron gate ahead, which the Mara unlocked and pulled to the side, allowing us access into the prison.

"I'll be waiting here," he said.

I nodded and followed Blaze inside. The cellblocks spread out around us in the huge cylindrical space. Correction Officers patrolled each level and the narrow passageways linking different sides. Hopeless whimpers and moans trickled out from the cages below on the ground level, sending chills down my spine.

We made it to the bottom, where the tunnels awaited, completely sealed with thick blocks of limestone.

"Well, good to see they held up their end of the bargain and closed off the tunnels," I muttered, and got the charmed satchels out of my backpack.

"It was in their best interests, after all," Blaze replied. He then took a compass out from his back pocket and flipped it open. "Okay, let's do east first, since it's right here."

We moved closer to the wall to our right. Blaze used a metal pick he'd brought with him from upstairs to carve a hole through the stone, while I carefully looked around. Fiona had left our side, looking for Demios.

I paid close attention to the Correction Officers, noticing their stern and somewhat concerned expressions as their eyes followed us around. They were most likely on edge, after the explosions—not that they'd been the friendliest dudes the day before, but still, I had to give them the benefit of the doubt.

They'd lost dozens of Maras and Imen up there; surely they weren't used to such a high number of casualties. Some of the victims could very well be family members.

I couldn't shake the uneasy feeling that the prison gave me, though. The moans of nearby prisoners kept tying my stomach up in knots. I caught glimpses of their profiles in different cages. From what I could tell, the bottom level was for the worst offenders, comprised of small and seemingly uncomfortable iron cages, while the cells above provided more space and even single beds for the inmates.

"I wonder what they're in here for," I mumbled, holding the charmed satchels in my hands.

"Probably thieves, murderers, and traitors," Blaze replied, somewhat absently, as he carved a hole deep enough for one of the satchels. "I have a hard time thinking they're all innocent."

"I don't doubt you're right." I sighed as he took one of the charm bags and shoved it into the hole. "I'm just wondering what got them here in the first place. I mean, Arrah said her brother was innocent, for example. He was accused of treason, conspiring against the city, but they didn't give any details. They just hauled his butt to jail…"

"Fair enough. That's one guy who might not belong here. What about the rest of them?" He glanced at me, his hands busy covering the satchel in the hole with the chunks of rock he'd carved out. "I mean, people of all species commit crimes. It's obviously in our natures—be we dragons, fae, vampires, or humans. As members of GASP, we've seen it over and over. Then we got here and… Well, it's the same."

"Do you think they deserve to die, though?"

I wanted to better understand Blaze. He offered viewpoints that were dramatically simple, but very honest. He wasn't a man of many words, but the thoughts he *did* voice, he dispensed carefully and eloquently. I liked that about him.

"I don't know." He shook his head slowly. "I don't think any of us are capable of determining who deserves to die and who doesn't. I've killed plenty of creatures so far. but they were all trying to kill us first... Self-defense, you know? But these people here? I doubt it. I bet they're already paying for their crimes."

Blaze had a point. Even if Arrah was right and her brother was, indeed, innocent, we couldn't be sure about the other prisoners. Maybe they did deserve to be behind bars. Then again, maybe they didn't. With everything else that was going on in this city, the Exiled Maras' legal system was slipping farther down to the bottom of our priorities list.

I only hoped that the charmed satchels would work this time around. After the attack on the Lords' mansions, we desperately needed a win against the daemons, even if it was in the form of a protective spell.

Too many lives depended on us, including our own.

7

BLAZE

We moved over to the south side of the prison, occasionally looking around at the cages in the middle. Most of the prisoners were Imen of different ages, but I'd seen a couple of Maras, too. They were all chained, dirty, and weak, barely moving, and their eyes had sunk into their heads.

I carved a hole into the southern wall, while Caia kept me company. The Correction Officers didn't seem very happy to see us, but I'd already gotten used to their natural reluctance toward outsiders. It was mostly a cultural thing, from what I could tell. However, they had no choice but to let us do our jobs —we were trying to protect them, too, after all.

"I still find it weird how fast the daemons moved to plant those explosives," Caia murmured.

Once I was done with the hole, she handed me another satchel.

"That is, if the daemons *were* behind this attack," I replied. Frankly, I wasn't convinced. Sure, the prison was suspicious, but not suspicious enough to make me think less of the Exiled Maras. But the timing just didn't fit.

"You think someone else did it?" She raised her eyebrows, and I needed a second to pull myself out of the deep teal pools of her eyes. Caia was simply mesmerizing.

"I wouldn't exclude the possibility just yet. Think about it this way: they had to have precise knowledge about the mansions and the servants' movements to be able to plant explosives in the Xunn mansion. Based on our last study of their patterns—at least before we met Tobiah and Sienna—the daemons were barely expanding their hunting grounds up to the second level of the city. As far as we know, Tobiah was the only daemon to reach the top floor, and he's been keeping his distance since he took Sienna. Maybe the daemons had inside help."

"Who do you think would be willing to assist the very creatures trying to kill them?" she asked, as I covered the hole. We walked along the edge of the wall until we reached the western side.

The Correction Officers' eyes followed us around as they patrolled the higher levels.

"Maybe someone who had a bone to pick with the Lords themselves." I shrugged, then stopped and carved another hole. "We know there are rebel Imen living on the other side of the gorge. Maybe they have loved ones here. Maybe they can't get back to each other because of the Exiled Maras, for example. It's just a shot in the dark, but you never know. Or maybe even the Exiled Maras themselves. What if they have some deal going on with the daemons that we know nothing about?"

"That's highly unlikely." Caia rejected the premise without hesitation. "Scratch that. It's downright impossible. They killed Darius and dozens of Maras in the process. Even if they were conspiring with the daemons—and, by default, shamelessly lying to us—they wouldn't kill their own. No, this was definitely aimed at the Exiled Maras. And frankly, given the tunnels leading up to the higher levels of the mountain... I'm thinking maybe the daemons have been lurking around those parts for longer than we initially presumed. Maybe they've been studying the Maras and spying on them for months, even years."

"That might explain how they had such knowledge of the mansions in the first place." I nodded as she handed me the third satchel. Our fingers touched, and an electric tingle rushed through my arms, heating me up on the inside.

She had a fascinating effect on me. There was something between us, though I'd yet to formulate coherent thoughts about it. I could feel our chemistry, as it thickened the air whenever we were close to each other. Caia kept me on high alert and had even slipped into my dreams. But my celibacy oath took precedence. I didn't want to put her through the ordeal of waiting around for me. It wasn't fair to her.

At the same time, I could feel my resolve slowly withering

away as we orbited around one another like two neutron stars about to collide and explode into a sea of light. The more time I spent near her, the more I disliked my paternal heritage. The oath had made sense to me when I took it.

To be fair, it still did. But something tugged at my heart, pulling me closer to Caia, and all I could think of was losing myself in her fire. I bit my lower lip and focused on covering the western hole, pushing the rubble in to cover the satchel.

"It does make sense." Caia continued our conversation, though I did catch the tremor in her voice. I affected her as much as she did me, and she wasn't very good at hiding it, either. I found that endearing, and it made me fall even deeper. "If they already knew what the key spots in the Xunn mansion were, along with the movements of Iman servants, the daemons could have easily performed an in-and-out operation to plant the explosives."

"Which would mean that their advancement to the second level of the city only relates to their hunting practices, not their actual knowledge of the city. So, in a way, the attack was their way of telling us not to underestimate them," I concluded, and couldn't stop myself from smiling at her. "You're brilliant, did you know that?"

Caia stared at me, her cheeks blossoming a beautiful pink. My heart faltered as liquid fire pulled through me. This girl was going to really put me to the test, and she didn't even know it. I took a deep breath and let it out slowly, trying to get my senses back under control, then carved the last hole into the northern side of the prison wall.

"Thank you, I guess?" she replied softly, her lips stretching into a smile.

There were two ways I could see this ending. Caia was intense, and I knew she would set me on fire—even in a literal sense, if I ever crossed her. This chemistry between us would either fizzle out or make me break my celibacy oath. I doubted I'd ever be able to hold onto any half-measure with her.

Her voice alone was enough to make my whole body buck and accumulate pressure, and I feared that only her kiss, her touch, would be able to free me. After that, I knew I wouldn't be able to stop. Judging by the way her pupils flared whenever I got close to her, I had a feeling she'd be right there with me.

"Okay, we're done here," I said, clearing my throat as I finished covering the fourth hole. "We're off to the top, right?"

"Yup." She nodded and walked back to the metal stairs leading up to the iron gate we'd come through. "Not sure there are any walls left for us to paint, but four trees pointing north, south, east, and west will do the trick."

The Correction Officer who had escorted us down to the prison straightened his back when he saw us. He'd been leaning against a nearby wall, looking rather lost. They were all affected by the explosion—some more than others.

"Where to next?" he asked us.

There was a willingness to be around us glimmering in his eyes. I hadn't noticed it before. He, like all the other Maras working for Lord Kifo, did his best to keep his emotions to himself. But he seemed to warm up to us, in his own way. I figured our presence helped dampen the anxiety that had probably permeated his facade in the wake of the attack.

"Upstairs to the top level," I replied. "We need to repaint some warding symbols."

He nodded and went up the spiral staircase. It was a long way to the Lords' mansions, but I still had plenty of adrenaline coursing through me since the explosions. I looked over my shoulder and noticed Caia staring at me, her eyes wide and filled with thoughts I wished I could understand.

We followed the Correction Officer up the stairs, leaving Fiona down in the prison to look for Demios. She knew where to find us afterward, anyway. I took Caia's hand in mine somewhere along the way. Her skin felt warm and soft against mine, soothing my very soul. She didn't seem to mind, either.

8

FIONA

(DAUGHTER OF BENEDICT & YELENA)

I had enough invisibility paste in my system for about one hour, plus two equal reserves in my backpack—one for me, and one for Demios, provided I found him. It took me a while to familiarize myself with the prison layout, especially with the cages on the bottom level.

Blaze and Caia left with the Correction Officer, while I continued to check every cage. The search process gave me an opportunity to get a better look at the prisoners. They all looked malnourished, weak, and simply out of their minds. Some were unconscious, lying on their bellies. Iron cuffs restricted their movements, the rough, unpolished metal digging into their bony ankles and wrists. Most of them had been in there for weeks, months, even years, but a couple seemed rather new to the "party" and had slightly more alert eye movements.

I had a feeling they'd be more useful to me than the others. Looking through the entire prison for Demios was going to take more than one hour, if I relied solely on myself. It couldn't hurt to ask one of the inmates.

There was one, in particular, who caught my eye. A young Iman male, maybe in his early twenties. His brown clothes were tattered and dusty, and the wounds on his bare shins and fore-arms were scabbing. He glanced around, exuding an air of hopelessness that gave me a mild stomachache. I moved closer to his cage, and noticed his blue eyes—pupils strangely dilated. Based on what Heron had told me about the side effects of mind-bending, this Iman was definitely under the Mara influence.

I couldn't reveal myself, but I needed to talk to him.

Here goes nothing...

"Please don't be alarmed," I said slowly.

The Iman's head shot up, then turned left and right, his eyes wide as the color drained from his face.

"I'm right here," I whispered, stepping forward. "You can't see me because I'm cloaked."

"Da... da... daemon..." He was horrified, slowly slipping to the back of his cage. His mouth opened as he prepared to scream from the bottom of his lungs.

Of course he thinks I'm a daemon. I'm freakin' invisible!

"No, no, no, I'm not a daemon! Please, please be quiet," I breathed, my voice trembling. "I'm here because I need to find my friend. I'm not going to hurt you, I promise. I would've already, if I wanted to."

He breathed heavily, almost hyperventilating, as he processed my words. He exhaled deeply, his shoulders dropping as he concluded that, indeed, I wasn't going to hurt him. He was definitely more alert than the others, but still physically weakened.

"What... What do you want?" he mumbled, pulling his knees up to his chest, his cuffs jingling with each movement. "Who are you? How do I know you're not a daemon, just playing with my head?"

That last one was a stretch. Even he probably knew it, given how his voice pitched higher toward the end of the question.

"I'm definitely not a daemon because if I were, I'd literally be draining the life out of you, and you probably know that, after last night." I groaned, rolling my eyes. He couldn't see me, though, which was a shame. It would've made my statement a lot more dramatic. "I'm Fiona, and I'm using the same cloaking spell that the daemons are using."

"How... How did you get it?" He blinked several times, visibly dazed.

"That's a long story. What's your name?"

"Merin," he replied, not sure where to look, since he could see right through me.

"Merin, why are you in prison?" I asked, trying to get the ball rolling, as I noticed him slowly loosening up.

"I... I stole gold from a Mara lady," he sighed, guilt drawing shadows on his pale face. He wrapped his arms around his calves, pulling his legs closer to his chest. "I don't know how long I'll be here... A few months, maybe a year... If I live that long."

"Why wouldn't you live through it? Are they hurting you in here?"

His bitter chuckle made me rethink my question. He looked terrible, obviously not the recipient of any five-star treatment.

This is prison, Fiona. And it's not your world. Focus!

I would've made a fantastic human rights campaigner, had I not been born and raised in The Shade.

"Did you not see those creatures trying to kill us last night?" he muttered, resting his forehead on his knees. "Not that I could see them, per se... but I could hear them. The others screaming and crying out in agony... They didn't reach my cage, but the others behind you... they didn't stand a chance..."

I glanced over my shoulder and saw the empty cages—six of them, to be precise, the iron bars bent, the locks broken, and the shackles discarded in a corner.

"What happened to the bodies?" I asked.

"The Correction Officers took them away, I guess... I don't know, I'm mostly sleeping these days..."

"Merin, I don't think the daemons will come back," I told him. "We've sealed the tunnels, and we put a protection spell over the city. Hopefully last night was the last time you will see them."

He shrugged, then let a sigh roll out of his chest. I couldn't help but feel sorry for him, though he deserved to be in here. You're supposed to pay for your crimes, after all.

"Hopefully," he echoed.

"How did you know about the daemons? How did you know they're called daemons?" I asked.

"They've been... part of our folklore for ages," he murmured, staring blankly ahead. His tone felt a bit automated. "They're evil and big, with red eyes and long claws... and they eat your soul."

"Was last night the first time you saw them, so to speak?"

Merin blanked out for a moment, as if looking for the memory. He shook his head.

"I... I think so. I'd remember it. Right?"

"Why are you asking me? Were you mind-bent?" I replied.

"Would I know if I was mind-bent?" The corner of his mouth twitched. Yeah, he was definitely mind-bent, and I wasn't going to get much out of him regarding the prison.

"That makes sense... sort of," I muttered. "Listen, Merin, I need your help. If you can, that is. I'm looking for my friend Demios. Arrah's brother? He worked in the Roho mansion. Do you, by any chance, know him?"

"Mm-hm..." He nodded slowly. "Most of the Imen my age know Demios. He used to be such a rascal when we were kids. One time, he almost burned down the White Star Hotel by accident, and we—"

"Merin, I'm in a bit of a rush here," I interrupted him. On any other occasion, I probably would've endured one or two childhood memories, but my clock was ticking. I was maybe fifteen minutes away from needing a refill on my invisibility spell, and I had to be in Demios's presence when that happened, so he could see me. "Do you know where they're keeping him?"

"I do," he said, pointing up above his head. "They let the inmates from above out once in a while, for ten minutes. He came by to see me. He'd heard me scream when they first brought me down here, begging to be reformed, not jailed. I wasn't that lucky..."

Merin's attention span was downright dismal.

"Where are they keeping him?" I persisted.

"Up on the third level," he conceded. "Cell number twenty, he told me. As if I could do anything with that information while I'm stuck down here..."

"Well, turns out you just did something with it right now." I wished he could see me smile. "Thank you, Merin, you've been really helpful. I promise I'll speak to the Correction Officers in charge and see if we can get your sentence reduced or something."

I was being honest. Of course, I wouldn't tell them about how he helped me get to Demios, since I was going to break Arrah's brother out of jail. But I was definitely going to speak to Lord Kifo about it... Maybe make up a little story about how he provided important information regarding last night's daemon attack. Whatever worked.

"Thank you," Merin replied, tears glazing his eyes as he pressed his lips tightly together.

"Hang in there," I whispered, then left him and snuck up the metal stairs leading to the cellblocks above.

I walked past a Correction Officer, then checked the top side of the cells as I moved forward. *Number five... ten... fifteen... twenty.*

There was a young Iman lying in his scruffy single bed, staring at the ceiling. His facial features were the only thing he had in common with Arrah. His eyes were dark brown, and his hair was long and black as a crow's feather. I found the striking difference between Demios and his sister quite odd; Arrah had a beautiful pair of pale green eyes and light brown hair.

I fumbled through my pockets for my lock-picking tool. It was a simple metal object resembling a very slim nail file. I couldn't see what I was doing, but this wasn't my first lock—nor was it going to be my last. My fingers worked on instinct until I heard the much-needed click, and I slowly pushed the cell door open.

Demios shot up into a seated position, his eyes wide with fear. Since he couldn't see me yet, I could only imagine the horror going through his head, as he probably expected to get his soul eaten or something.

"Please don't scream or anything," I whispered, and pulled the cell door shut behind me, careful not to make any unnecessary noise. "I'm not a daemon. I'm not here to hurt you, I promise."

He raised his eyebrows and gave me a brief nod. I realized then that he was looking right at me. I glanced down and noticed the invisibility spell fading away, revealing me.

"I can see that now... That you're not a daemon, I mean," Demios replied. "They're ugly, scary beasts..."

"You've seen them, too?" I felt my jaw drop.

"Only in books." He shrugged and moved to the side of his bed. His pupils were also dilated, but he seemed much calmer, more composed than Merin. A better sight than the Imen in the other cages, too. "I heard them last night, but... I couldn't see them. Only white lights leaving the cages..."

"Oh... you witnessed the whole soul-eating part, then," I said, then flipped back into my state of urgency. It was only a matter of time before a Correction Officer passed by Demios's cell. I listened carefully to the footsteps, which were currently on the other side of the block. "Demios, I'm here to help you."

"Help me how?"

He's as blank as the other one...

"I'm going to get you out of here and take you to your sister," I replied, and took my little jar of invisibility paste out of my backpack, holding it out for him to see. "Eat half of this, and we'll be out of here in minutes."

"Wait... Wait... Hold on." Demios frowned, then shook his head. "I'm in prison. I committed a crime. I belong here."

"Are you sure about that?" I raised an eyebrow, somehow sensing exactly how deleted his brain was. Once more, Heron's accounts of extreme mind-bending came to mind, and Demios looked and sounded like an excellent example. His movements were slow, his responses even slower—not to mention the blank look on his face, the mild slur in his speech, and his dilated pupils, all signs of Mara intervention. He nodded, his lips parting as if his jaw couldn't keep up with the rest of his head. "Okay, why are you in prison, then?"

"I... I committed a crime..."

"What crime?"

"I... I... I think I..."

I could almost hear his train of thought derailing and crashing into a dark abyss. He had no idea why he'd been jailed in the first place. His brow furrowed as he scratched the back of his head, struggling to remember.

"That's what I thought," I muttered. "You've been mind-bent, Demios. You don't belong here. Your sister sent me. She knows you're innocent."

"You know my sister?"

"Yes, and I promised her I would help. Do you want to see Arrah again?" I asked. He nodded in response, so I gave him the jar. He took it with trembling fingers and stared at the shimmering paste inside for a moment, before he gave me a questioning look. "Eat half of that. It will make you invisible, like I was just now. I'll need the other half. Once we vanish, we'll be able to move freely and quietly get out of this place. They won't even know what happened to you."

The Correction Officer's steps seemed closer than before. I needed Demios to move fast, so I removed the lid from the jar and took his hand, helping him scoop out some of the paste. He finished the rest of the movement and swallowed the glimmering cream, his tongue clicking against the roof of his mouth. He cringed a little.

"Yeah, not exactly honey and plums, I know." I scoffed and consumed the rest of the jar before I put it back in my bag. No way was I leaving any evidence behind. I took Demios's hand and helped him up, then hooked his finger into one of my pockets. "Okay, we're about to vanish now. Whatever happens, do not let go of me, okay?"

Demios gazed at me with fascination. We were shimmering away, and disappeared before I heard the Correction Officer move forward on the other side. We still had about thirty seconds to get out without bumping into the Mara.

"Remember, Demios," I whispered. "Don't let go!"

"I won't let go," he breathed.

At least he was paying attention.

I fluffed up the raggedy pillows and sheets on Demios's bed, enough to make it look like he was still in bed—at least from a distant, casual angle. We then left the cell, and I carefully pulled the door shut behind me and put the lock back in place.

It would require an extra ounce of attention from a Correction Officer to notice something wrong in Demios's cell. If the universe worked in our favor, they wouldn't notice he was gone until morning, at least.

I took a deep breath, and we quietly slipped down the stairs, all the way to the bottom level. My heart was pounding in my chest, but I took comfort in the fact that Demios was still clinging to my pocket—he was obeying me, which was important if we wanted to get out of here in one piece and without triggering any alarms, or, worse, some massive Iman-hunt...

We reached the gate through which Caia and Blaze had come through. I picked the lock, then gently opened it, and went through, frequently looking over my shoulder to make sure no one was looking our way. Fortunately, the Correction Officers were scattered above, their backs to us.

I closed the gate behind us, and then went up the stairs. About two minutes in, I could hear Demios breathing heavily. It was a long way up, and he didn't have the physical strength to keep up with my usual speed.

"I'm guessing we'll have to take a couple of breaks along the way." I sighed. "It's a long way up, my friend."

"It's... It's okay... I can do it... But yeah... Breaks... I need... I need a break..."

Demios was already out of breath. I stretched my neck around, bracing myself for a slightly longer trip back to the top. It was either that or carry him on my back, and I didn't want it to get to that just yet.

I'd had a long freaking day already, and I was exhausted. That bed at the Broken Bow Inn was already on my mind. And so was Zane and my experience as his prisoner. Weirdest six or seven hours in my life.

"Ready to go?" I asked, eager to drop him off at the South

Bend Inn, where his sister was checked in, along with the other Lords' servants.

The sooner I got Arrah on our side, the quicker I could just sink into a bed and black out for a few hours. Demios didn't answer.

"Demios?"

"Yes?"

"Are you ready?" I reformulated my question.

"Yes, I nodded yes..."

"I can't see you, buddy." I almost stifled a grin before I remembered he couldn't see me either. "Let's go."

We kept moving. It wasn't long before he needed another break.

By the third pause, however, I groaned with frustration and grabbed him, tossing him over my shoulder like a bag of potatoes. He whimpered for a while, but eventually got accustomed to being carried up hundreds of stairs.

"You're strong," he croaked at one point.

Indeed, I was. But I was also very tired. Every minute that passed made me cry out for my bed. The adrenaline was finally leaving my body, and exhaustion was slowly settling in.

Just a little more, Fi. Just a bit.

9

FIONA

(DAUGHTER OF BENEDICT & YELENA)

After we reached the third level of the city, we made our way up to the seventh, where the South Bend Inn was. The building was quite large, nestled between cobblestone alleys, with a dark green tile roof and white walls. Judging by the size, it probably housed over one hundred rooms, and the lights were on in most of them. The inn was almost full, given the sudden influx of Imen servants from the five Lords' mansions, which meant I had to scour through the reception registry for Arrah's name and room number.

I set Demios down on his feet and he resumed his grip on my pocket. "Don't let go, Demios," I whispered as we approached the inn's front entrance.

There were many Imen and Maras out, all of them wearing looks of grief and concern on their faces. At least three hours had passed since the attack. The wounds were still fresh, and rumors buzzed around the scattered crowd. I caught snippets of various conversations, and they all revolved around who could've done such a horrible thing, and why. The word "daemons" came up several times, along with "It can't be!" and "How can they be real?" The people of the city were clearly in the dark, but had a faint idea as to what was going on.

I felt Demios still tugging my pocket as we slipped past the Imen gathered in front of the entrance. We snuck through the spacious lobby and made it behind the reception desk. The Iman in charge, a young female in a simple black dress with long sleeves and brown hair caught up in a tight bun, was busy explaining the inn's policies to an elderly couple.

She had her back to the registry—a large, leather-bound book with brownish pages. I quickly flipped through it, until I found Arrah's name listed at the bottom.

Room forty-three.

We then went up the stairs to the second floor, and made our way down the hallway until we found room number forty-three. I glanced around, checking to see if anyone was close enough to hear us. There were several Imen at the end, coming down from the third floor, but too far away to hear us.

I knocked on the door, and, less than half a minute later, Arrah opened it. There were traces of soot on her face, and parts of her service dress had been burnt, but she was okay from what I could tell at first glance.

"Sister!" Demios's voice erupted from my side.

Crap, no! Too soon.

Arrah was startled and looked around, visibly confused. I found Demios's hand gripping my pocket and pulled him inside the room, shushing him in the process. Arrah yelped, then turned around, her greenish eyes wide with shock and fear.

"Arrah, don't be scared; it's me, Fiona," I said gently, standing in the middle of her room. "You can't see me yet, but I'm here, and so is your brother."

"Wha... What?" she managed, then quickly looked over her shoulder at the hallway, and shut the door behind her, locking it for good measure. "What's happening? Why can't I see you? Demios?"

"I'm here, Sister," he replied.

"We're using an invisibility spell. It should wear off soon," I added.

"Demios?" Arrah's face lit up.

I felt him let go of my pocket. Arrah gasped, held her arms out, then smiled and put them around an invisible Demios. They were hugging. She burst into tears, sighing with relief as she felt her brother's embrace.

"How... How is this possible?" she croaked, relaxing in Demios's arms.

The spell started to wear off, revealing us with a fading shimmer. *Perfect timing.*

"We have some tricks up our sleeves." I winked, as Arrah could finally see me. "As you can see, I managed to get your brother out of prison."

They held each other, and Arrah gradually regained her composure, wiping tears and swallowing back another round. She held his face in her hands, frowning as she briefly checked his expression, his eyes, and his overall look. Demios was quiet, sporting a blank half-smile that further confirmed her suspicions.

"He's been severely mind-bent," she murmured, then stared at me. "They really did a number on him, didn't they?"

"I think so. I'm sorry." I shrugged, leaning against a wooden cabinet by the wall facing her bed. It was a simple room, with modest but sturdy furniture and a floral-patterned bedspread. "He doesn't even remember what he did to get himself imprisoned."

"Oh, Demios," she breathed, shifting her focus back to her brother.

"I'm okay now. I'm with you," he said.

She guided him over to the bed and pushed him into a seated position, then turned to face me.

"I have to get him out of here. I need to get him as far away from this city and the Maras as possible," she said.

"Do you intend to go beyond the gorges, to the western plains, by any chance?" I asked.

"I can't go anywhere while the daemons are out and prowling around the city." She shook her head, giving her brother a sideways glance. Demios was quite lethargic, his shoulders down and his eyes droopy. "I'll have to hide him somewhere in the city until we can both leave safely... though I don't know when that will be..."

"Do you have a place in mind?"

"A couple of my father's old friends might be able to help, yes." She pursed her lips, running her fingers through Demios's long hair. He closed his eyes and let himself fall back, instantly dozing off. "They've turned his brain into mush... It will take months, maybe years to fix him..."

"Can you fix mind-bending?" I replied, wondering how that could possibly work. I'd never heard of anyone, other than the Mara who had originally inflicted the mind-bending, being able to undo it.

"It's not easy, but yes," Arrah explained briefly. "It doesn't always work, though. It's a longshot, and it's painful and time consuming, but it's worth a try. My brother is a bright young Iman. He doesn't deserve to be reduced to... this."

I walked over to the window, checking the crowd still gathered outside. They were all restless, whispering to one another while giving the nearby Correction Officers some fearful looks. Some looked hopeful, though—as if Lord Kifo's people really could keep them safe. All I could do in that moment was hope that the protection spell would work the second time around, and that Arrah would be able to fill in some of the gaps in our knowledge about Azure Heights and its inhabitants.

"Arrah, we've kept our end of the bargain, as you can see," I said. "In fact, we've done a lot more. We got you your brother back. I need you to come through for us and tell us what's going on here. You know more than you've told us; there's no point denying it."

"I'm not going to deny it," Arrah replied, then pointed at her brother. "I need to take Demios to safety. Once he's hidden and out of reach, I will come to you, and I will tell you everything I know. I promise!"

"Why can't we talk now?"

"Because my brother is still here. He could be sleeping, or he could be pretending." She shuddered. "If they mind-bent him, it means he's susceptible to various commands, including subconsciously spying on me, or worse. He wouldn't even know it. I can't put you or anyone else in danger, and I have to keep him safe. So, I'll take him somewhere in the city where no one can find him. He'll be restrained and be given a first treatment to break the mind-bending effect he's under. Then, and only then, will I be able to speak freely."

Partly satisfied with the result of my endeavor to reunite Demios with his sister in exchange for information, I took a deep breath and walked over to the door.

"Arrah, please don't let us down," I said. "Come talk to me as soon as you get your brother to safety. I don't want us to go into enemy territory without potentially life-saving information again. It nearly got us killed."

Arrah gave me a brief nod, paired with a reassuring smile.

"I promise. Give me until tomorrow night," she replied. "I'll find him a place by then, for sure."

"Okay," I agreed, then unlocked the door and walked out.

The inn was bustling with people, as dozens were returning to their rooms. I took advantage of the crowded hallways and staircases, and made my way out without any curious heads turning to give me a second glance.

At least Demios was safe, and Arrah was ready to talk. I considered that fantastic progress, given the overall mess and the permanent feeling of taking three steps forward and two steps back all the time.

10

HARPER

(DAUGHTER OF HAZEL & TEJUS)

W e were pretty much done with combing through the explosion site for any useful evidence. There wasn't much else to work with, though, besides the half-molten detonator chunks we'd found in the Xunn and Kifo mansions. Nothing to point in a specific direction, anyway.

"Only one question remains at this point," I said, as Avril, Heron, Scarlett, and Caspian gathered around me. "The ephelis sticks. Where did they get them from?"

Caspian raised an eyebrow, looking down at the city unraveling below. His gaze focused somewhere on the staircase leading up to us. I followed it and turned around to see a Correction Officer coming up—he was the Mara who had been sent down to check on Master Dresdel, their craftsman of sorts. He didn't look very happy.

"I think we'll get our answer now," Caspian muttered, then gave the Correction Officer a brief nod. "What did Master Dresdel say?"

"Nothing, milord. He's dead," the Mara replied, his brow furrowed.

Caspian's aura caught a vibrant shade of red as he processed the information. I could see the anger almost flowing through his limbs, down to his hands as they balled into fists. The muscle in his jaw began to twitch.

"What do you mean, he's dead?" Caspian asked, his teeth grinding as he struggled to keep his cool.

"He was killed, milord. I found him dead on the floor of his workshop. His head was cut off, and his ephelis reserves were ransacked," the Correction Officer explained.

I would've lied if I'd said I didn't see this coming. Looking back, it kind of made sense. Whoever was behind the attack had clearly procured the explosives from the only known source. Silencing said source was the logical next step, as grim as that sounded.

"Are you able to estimate time of death?"

"No longer than twenty hours, milord," the Mara replied.

"And no less than what?" I interjected, trying to work Master Dresdel's death into our already-strange timeline.

"Twelve, judging by stiffness, milady."

"Gah, seriously, this is making less sense now!" I groaned, rolling my eyes in exasperation. Caspian and the rest of my team watched quietly as I paced back and forth along the edge of the terrace. "We came back from the gorges about eight, maybe nine hours ago. Which means that Master Dresdel was already dead. The math just doesn't work out. Were they already preparing for the attack at the time? It's the only logical explanation!"

"What if the explosions had nothing to do with what we did in the Valley of Screams?" Scarlett offered, hands resting on her hips. "What if Harper is right, and they were already preparing to hit the city before we even went into the gorges?"

"By 'they' you mean the daemons?" Avril asked.

"There's no other group of suspects available at this point, is there?" Scarlett replied.

"Okay, so how does that help us going forward?" I sighed, then stilled as Caia and Blaze joined us on the top level. "You guys okay?"

"Yeah, just repainting the symbols for Patrik." Caia lifted the paint can in her hands to show me, as she and Blaze came closer. "What have you got so far from here?"

"A stinking mess, it seems," Heron concluded. "To summarize, the explosions were not retaliation for our stint in the gorges. The explosives were stolen from a local craftsman. He was killed while we were still out there, so the timeline's a bit fuzzy."

I slowly raised my hands to stop the conversation from going any further. We needed to brief Hansa, Patrik, and Jax as soon as possible. These findings could have an impact on our strategy going forward. And we also needed to get some sleep.

"Listen, let's go back to the infirmary and brief the others on all this," I said, gripping the back of my neck with one hand to relieve some of the tension. My muscles felt as though they were carved from stone. "The sooner we do this, the quicker we can get some shut-eye. I'm feeling broken, and will come apart if I don't get some Z's..."

"Harper's right." Heron nodded, then patted Blaze on the shoulder. "We'll leave you two to finish the whole protection spell mojo, and see you downstairs in a bit."

I walked past Caspian, my hand brushing against his.

"I'll see you tomorrow," he said slowly, and I looked over my shoulder, nearly melting when his eyes found mine. That warmth was so strange and unfamiliar, yet so wonderful, it nearly eclipsed the horror of everything that had happened up to this point.

"See you," I mumbled, not sure what else to say. He baffled me.

We headed back to the infirmary, where Jax, Hansa, and Patrik were going over the gorge map. Avril and Heron briefed them on their findings from the mansions' ruins, and I broke the news about the Maras' craftsman:

"Master Dresdel was killed and his workshop ransacked. They looted his ephelis reserve. So, at least the source of the explosives used is confirmed. The weird part is that Master Dresdel got his head cut off sometime between twelve and twenty hours ago."

Jax, Hansa, and Patrik gave each other a round of confused looks.

"Wait, that doesn't make sense." Hansa frowned. "It doesn't fit our timeline."

"Yup," I replied. "It means they were already planning and preparing the attack, long before we got back from the gorges."

"So it wasn't retaliation," Jax concluded.

"Not for what we did earlier." I shrugged. "Maybe for the ass-kicking they got the night before when they broke into the prison, I'm thinking..."

"Either way, that was vicious. It also confirms our earlier suspicions," Hansa said. "The daemons definitely know this city and its operations inside out. They knew how to infiltrate the Lords' mansions without anyone noticing an explosive device. They knew about Master Dresdel's ephelis reserve. I can't help but wonder what else they know..."

"I need some sleep before I can try to answer that question," I muttered, leaning against the window frame. My muscles were starting to liquefy, and my neck was quite stiff. Normally my stamina covered two to three days with no sleep, easily, but after the constant fighting since the night Fiona was taken, I needed a breather.

Caia and Blaze returned shortly afterward, followed by Fiona, who briefed us on Arrah and the successful extraction of her brother, Demios. *Finally, a small win for our side...*

"She promised she'll find me by tomorrow night." Fiona completed her account of Demios's rescue and return to his sister. "Once he's safe and hidden, Arrah will be able to talk to us. She feared her brother might have been mind-bent into spying on his own people, if released from prison, from what I understood."

"Whoa, that's some serious conspiracy stuff," I exclaimed, finding it hard to imagine such a scenario after I'd seen Mara bodies being carried out of the rubble upstairs.

"We won't know for sure until she speaks up," Patrik said. "In the meantime, let's set up a proper spell to protect this city. Caia, Blaze, all done on your end, right?"

"Absolutely," Caia replied with a smirk. "We repainted the symbols around the Lords' mansions, too. But we used trees this time, just to be sure."

"Thank you both," the Druid replied, and moved to the area in the middle of the room that had the spell paraphernalia and drawings prepared. He chanted the spell in a low voice and clapped his hands once, releasing an energy pulse. Golden light burst out of his body and spread out, disappearing beyond the walls of the infirmary. "I used samples from the daemon and the pit wolf collars to specify the threat that the spell needs to keep out."

We all stood there, quiet for a while, enjoying the silence.

Jax then opened the door, calling out to the Correction Officers stationed outside:

"You there! Tell Lord Kifo that the protection spell is in place to cover the prison, too. However, you should have officers on the second and third floors for the rest of the night." He then shifted his focus back to us, running a hand through his short black hair. "I'll need all of us to get some sleep through what's left of the night. We're all pretty drained, judging by Harper's face."

His smirk made me straighten my back and cross my arms over my chest, exuding faux offence.

"Hah, speak for yourself," I quipped.

"We have a route set up for the gorges tomorrow, but I trust Lord Kifo will be able to offer some valuable input after the funerals," Jax continued. "We'll meet back here at eight, as the procession starts at nine, from what Emilian told us. It'll give us an hour to hash out details, let the Druid dispose of the daemon corpse, and prepare for what comes next."

"To reiterate," Hansa added, "Jax, Blaze, Caia, Harper, Lord Kifo, and I will infiltrate the gorges again tomorrow, after the funerals. The plan is to find and capture a daemon in there, and force him to reveal one of the access routes into their underground cities. Lord Kifo might be able to help with that, too. We'll find out more once we have him all to ourselves."

"And the rest of us will stay here." Fiona nodded. "Understood. That being said, I would like to speak to Cynara sometime soon. Preferably tomorrow."

"The servant girl from our first dinner with the Lords?" I asked, remembering the young Iman female and her fragile state, along with Hera, her sister.

"Yes. I'm hoping we can get some more information out of her," Fiona replied, "about anything... Avril, Heron, would you be able to join me for this? I'm hoping we could maybe bypass some of her mind-bending blocks. Surely she must have some. It could lead to nothing, but then again, with so many questions we have yet to answer, she might surprise us... I don't know."

"That makes sense," Heron replied. "I mean, like you said, it's worth a shot. Worst-case scenario her brain is already mush, but we won't know until we try. It's a useful way to kill time while Jax and his team check the underground cities."

"I agree," Avril chimed in. "Speaking to Cynara could at least help us understand the extent of mind-bending in this city. After all, there is only so much that the Exiled Maras can justify as psychological treatment and forcing confessions out of criminals. It would be good to put the issue to rest, once and for all, especially after what happened tonight. Despite the warning signs, I'm finding it increasingly difficult to believe that the Maras have anything to do with the disappearances and the daemons. If anything, the Imen seem to know more about these creatures than anyone else."

"Well, the Imen and Lord Kifo," I muttered.

"Yeah, but he's a very odd exception, and I'm hoping he'll be willing to tell us more about it as soon as he gets the chance," Hansa offered, then took a deep breath and glanced at each of us. "Okay, time to go to bed!"

We left the infirmary, with Patrik last. He locked the door and placed another protection spell on the building. I looked out onto the gorges in the distance and froze. Using my True Sight for just a little bit of a zoom, I could see the red eyes clearly—flickering defiantly in the absolute darkness of the limestone ravines.

"Hey, guys," I breathed, "can you look out over there and tell me what you see?"

I kept my eyes on the Valley of Screams, determined not to let those red dots out of my sight this time. One by one, my teammates joined my side, following my gaze. Their eyes narrowed for a moment, then popped wide open.

"Lots of daemons out there tonight, I see," Hansa growled, twisting her lips with disgust.

"Ah, so I'm not imagining this. Okay," I muttered.

"No, and I am sorry we doubted you the other night." Hansa gently nudged my shoulder with hers. "They're getting more brazen now."

"Hopefully GASP will be here soon," Jax added. "We need more than one dragon to launch a serious offensive against the daemons. And that will be either to obliterate them or force them into some kind of armistice."

"Speaking of which," Blaze interjected, frowning slightly, "it's been a few days, and GASP has yet to come for us. They obviously can't reach us via Telluris—shouldn't they be flying out here by now?"

"I don't know, Blaze," Jax replied, shaking his head slowly as he gazed at the red eyes in the distance. "I'm sure they'll be here shortly. Honestly, I'm too tired to pass any judgment on this right now. Let's sleep on it, and let's not forget that the asteroid belt is playing a crucial role in our communication and travel issues. Maybe they're dealing with the same."

Not fully satisfied with that idea, Blaze shrugged and headed up the stairs toward the Broken Bow Inn. The rest of the team followed, including myself. I kept glancing over my shoulder, the red eyes still watching.

My blood chilled and shivers ran down my spine. I cleared my throat and focused on the walk to the inn, going over everything that had happened throughout the day, while the others recounted their own versions of the events. There were different perspectives between us, but they all carried us forward toward our common goal—protecting those who could not defend themselves.

Our day so far had not been extraordinary, given the anti-climactic and yet explosive end. But we'd gotten Fiona back, and we'd killed scores of daemons back in the Valley of Screams. On top of that, we'd reset the protection spell over the city, and we'd even managed to snatch Demios out of prison, thanks to Fiona.

"Hey, Fiona." I remembered the question that had crossed my mind earlier, the one I'd forgotten to ask. She gave me a quick glance over her shoulder. "How long do you think before the Correction Officers realize that Demios is missing?"

"I think by late morning at best." She chuckled. "I ruffled his bed up. Made it look like he's sleeping. They'll probably serve him breakfast and notice something's off."

"What if they trace it back to us?" I asked. "Surely they'll figure out there was something supernatural involved…"

"They'll have to prove it before they even think of accusing us," Jax replied, confidence adding some extra weight to his husky voice. "And I doubt that will happen while we're out here, trying to keep *them* safe."

He had a point. The Exiled Maras had no proof that we had anything to do with it. Either way, as long as Demios was free and out of their reach, it didn't really matter. We finally had Arrah on our side. Soon enough, she would tell us more about the city and its people.

Looking around at passing Imen and Maras, I couldn't help but shiver briefly. Their picture-perfect lives were crumbling before their very eyes. Their love of art and fashion was obscured by blood and ashes. Yes, they were a complicated bunch… but they didn't deserve any of this.

11

SCARLETT

(DAUGHTER OF JERAMIAH & PIPPA)

Once we reached the Broken Bow Inn, we picked up some blood from the bar on our way up to our rooms. Given the night's events, the inn had decided to keep the bar open and offer us free blood.

"It's our way of thanking you for being here and trying to keep us safe," the Iman bartender had said, a sad smile crossing his face.

Patrik walked me to my room as we talked about the swamp witch magic we'd seen the daemons use. We stopped in front of my door, and I leaned against its frame, while he kept a couple of meters' distance from me.

"Once Jax and the others get inside the daemons' underground city, we'll probably understand more about where they got the swamp witch magic from in the first place," Patrik said, his hands behind his back.

"Yeah, I guess we don't have enough to go on right now." I nodded slowly, focusing my gaze on his face. His steely blue eyes drilled into me, but he wasn't doing it on purpose. I figured it came naturally to him. "What's important is that we know they have it and they're not afraid to use it. I guess what we need to determine next is how much swamp witch knowledge they have to work with."

"That's right. Again, I think that will be revealed during Jax's incursion into the gorges tomorrow," he replied, slowly moving forward.

I took a deep breath, trying to adjust to the shrinking space between us.

"In the meantime, we'll focus on the asteroid belt," I said.

A moment passed in silence. Patrik then gave me a half-smile. My heart skipped a beat.

"Thank you for all your help so far, Scarlett." His voice was soft, opposing the sharp blue in his eyes. "Especially in the gorges today. I'd be dead if it weren't for you."

"It's my pleasure." I tried to shrug it off, but he moved even closer, and my voice nearly disappeared. "I mean, it's what colleagues do, right? Besides, I enjoy working with you. I'm genuinely impressed by your craft, as I'm sure I've said before..."

"You have, but I won't get tired of it, just like I won't get tired of thanking you for saving me, since this is... what, the second time now?"

The corner of his mouth moved a little, as if a smile were working its way to the surface, but he stifled it. He came across as relaxed, though that could easily be interpreted as tiredness. Either way, it felt like a good time to ask what had been bugging me since the morning we'd found Minah's dead body in the infirmary.

"Patrik, I've been meaning to ask, but we haven't had a chance, given everything that's happened," I started, choosing my words carefully. "The other day, when we found Minah's body and Jax mind-bent you into remembering what had happened... you said you had a dream... and that I was in it. That at first you were dreaming about Kyana, and she then turned into... Well, she turned into me. Do you mind telling me what that was about?"

He stared at me for a while, and I waited patiently for his answer. A flurry of emotions trembled in his eyes, his brow furrowing slightly. He was taking his time formulating an answer, while I struggled to keep my pulse in check. Then a distant drumming sound caught my attention. Or at least, it seemed distant. It wasn't. It was right in front of me, nestled beneath Patrik's ribcage.

My vampire hearing was picking up on his heartbeat. Tumultuous, erratic, and thundering in his chest. He was nervous.

"It's been a couple of really crazy days, Scarlett," Patrik said, his voice calm, in stark contrast with his pulse. "To be honest, I'm having trouble making sense of what's happening in my head, not to mention my dreams... It's difficult to understand one's subconscious, and as much as I would like to, I don't think I can offer you an explanation. I think it just happened."

He looked a little tortured, as if he wanted to say more but couldn't—or worse, didn't know *what* to say. He'd never thought he'd mention a dream of me out loud, in front of the whole team. It couldn't be easy for him to actually talk about it.

Time to lighten things up a bit, then...

"Meh, it probably means you're getting the hots for me and your subconscious is trying to tell you that," I chuckled.

He almost laughed, his lips stretching into a grin. But then his serenity faded and he faltered for a second, his gaze softening as it settled on my face again. The humor rushed past us, and I suddenly felt naked in front of him, vulnerable and defenseless. His eyes lit up, and what I'd just joked about seemed to sink in.

It was all happening in slow motion, and I had a front-row seat, watching as Patrik took my weak attempt at a joke as something very serious, something he'd actually considered:

"I'm in mourning, Scarlett," he whispered. "I'm still learning to live without Kyana, and I'm getting the hang of it, you know..."

"I... I was joking, you know—"

"Don't think I don't see you, Scarlett," he went on, determined to make himself heard, and inched closer. I had to look up to maintain eye contact, and I had to work harder to keep my breathing under control, our lips mere inches apart. "I'm not blind. I'm aware of the effect that you have... The effect that you have on me, even when we're just standing next to each other. I just don't know what to do with that yet. But I want you to know that I *see* you."

I was simply floored. Out of words. My thoughts jammed in the back of my throat and my temperature spiked.

What... What do I do with this? What do I do with what he just said?

My lips parted, my mouth trying to form some words, but nothing came out. His gaze lowered, and I noticed a shadow settling in the blue pools of his eyes.

"Good night, Scarlett," he muttered, then walked away, disappearing into his room farther down the hall.

He left me with a spiked temperature and a riled-up heart muscle. He'd just said he saw me. He noticed me. As if... As if I were real, and more than a teammate.

I exhaled sharply and went into my room, locking the door behind me. A couple of minutes went by as I tried to make sense of the storm brewing inside me—a strange mixture of excitement and... curiosity. What did it all mean? What did *he* mean?

For the first time in months, I didn't feel like I was in a one-sided limbo anymore. Patrik had just acknowledged that he was aware of me, of the... effect I had on him.

Whoa.

My room was too hot. Or at least it felt that way. I went over to the window and opened it wide, gazing at the city spreading below with dark rooftops and alleys, thick tree crowns and twinkling street lamps.

There was so much to unpack in his statement. And I also needed to get some sleep.

"I'm screwed," I mumbled, realizing how powerful an impact Patrik had on me. It had already gone past the stage of an innocent crush. There was so much about him that I couldn't get enough of... I was falling for him, deeply and irreversibly. "I am so screwed..."

And the fact that there was the clear possibility of one fraction of my feelings being mutual—well, that certainly added a spring to my step. I had to give it time. He needed patience and understanding, more than anything. A friend. A teammate. Someone he could rely on. It would be me. It had to be me.

Movement somewhere below caught my eye. A passing shadow that crossed my field of vision. I caught a glimpse and followed it till it reached a dark cluster of large trees on the edge of the city level. My breath hitched as I realized what I was looking at.

"Holy hell," I breathed, feeling my eyes attempting to jump out of their sockets. "Holy friggin' hell..."

The pit wolf I'd rescued in the gorges had followed me all the way up here. I could see it clearly, resting at the base of a tree, out of sight on that level. Its glimmering red eyes were focused on me, its mouth open and tongue hanging out like it was a good dog.

What in the world...

For a moment I thought the city's protection spell hadn't worked, but I quickly shook the idea away, since the pit wolf didn't have a collar anymore. It was free. And it didn't strike me as evil or hostile, despite its frightening appearance.

It was just sitting there, watching me quietly. It didn't react. It didn't even growl or glare at the Imen who passed by, less than twenty feet away from it.

You giant weirdo...

Whatever it wanted from me, it didn't involve stringing my intestines out. That was clear. I wondered if the creature was maybe feeling thankful after I'd released it from its charmed collar.

I also had a feeling this wouldn't be the last time I'd see the pit wolf, and it didn't bother me. In fact, it kind of comforted me. On any other day, the presence of a giant beast waiting outside my window would have creeped the hell out of me.

But on Neraka... It was better to have a pit wolf keeping me company than invisible daemons lurking around, eager to slice me open and consume my soul.

12

HARPER

(DAUGHTER OF HAZEL & TEJUS)

The night went by in what felt like seconds. I remembered putting my head down, and then my eyes peeled open to find a solitary strand of sunshine slipping through the window shutters. A cold shower was needed to get myself back into a functioning mode—the past couple of days had definitely taken their toll on me.

After we went over mission details at the infirmary, we joined the rest of the people of Azure Heights on the fourth level, at the funeral home. Scarlett and Patrik stayed behind, as they had Minah's coffin to bring out into the procession and the daemon's body to burn.

Thousands of Maras and Imen stood quietly outside and in the alleys surrounding the simple, cubic white building. A plethora of beautiful flowers lined both sides of the procession path, leaving about twenty feet in between, and connecting the main entrance of the funeral home to the cemetery gates down below, on the north side of the mountain.

Candles burned inside, the scent of melted wax and jasmine filling my lungs. The terrace was covered, but we all wore black, as we were about to go into the sunlight for the burial ceremony. My team and I were in our usual black leather suits, with head covers, masks, and goggles ready to be put on once we left the safety of the awnings.

The Imen and Maras had opted for the same type of clothing—black cloaks, which made the crowd look downright eerie. They all held flowers in their arms, waiting patiently for the dozens of Imen and Maras killed in the attack to be carried out in their coffins.

The silence weighed heavy on our shoulders, but there was nothing we could say or do to make this easier. The people were in pain and mourning. Loss could not be reversed.

Caspian and the remaining three Lords came down, accompanied by Vincent, Rewa, Amalia, and the other family members who had survived the explosions. They, too, wore black cloaks and brought flowers with them. Caspian crossed the funeral path and came to stand next to me, his eyes searching my face. Emilian, Farrah, Rowan, Rewa, and the others waited on the other side.

"Did you sleep?" Caspian asked, his voice low. I gave him a brief nod. "You don't look like you slept."

Wow. Right before the funeral. Smooth...

"I'm fine," I muttered, rolling my eyes. I looked away. He stared at me for a while, somewhat confused.

"I didn't mean it as an insult," he whispered. "I just think you need more rest."

"Well, thank you for your concern, Lord Kifo, but I'm fine."

Music started playing inside, two flutes and two drums, complementing each other in a slow but steady rhythm. It was a song of heartbreak and sadness, trickling out of the funeral home and spreading around. It brought tears to people's eyes. Rewa was a mess, poor thing, her eyes red and puffy and her skin paler than usual. Vincent had his arm around her, holding her close and comforting her.

The crowd hummed as they all took out metal masks from the folds of their black cloaks—they were simple, made from meranium, with eye holes and molded noses and lips, similar to Venetian masks back on Earth. They all put them on and pulled the hoods over their heads. The music got louder.

The funeral home doors opened wide, and out came two drummers and flute players, followed by four elder Maras, four old Imen, and a string of coffins that seemed never-ending. They all wore black cloaks and meranium masks, spreading flower petals as they walked down the processional path.

I heard murmurs and sobs emerging from the crowd as more caskets were carried out on the shoulders of Imen. My stomach tightened when I allowed my inner sentry to "listen" to the emotions pouring out of the Imen surrounding us—there was so much grief... and angst, and fear.

The last coffin left the funeral home, an elegant black wooden box with gold lace motifs that held Darius. The cleric came out behind it, wearing a white hood and meranium mask and holding a scepter made of gold, with a cavity at the top, in which fragrant incense burned. Ten more Imen in black cloaks followed.

"Do they represent a cult or religion of sorts?" I asked Caspian, watching as the crowd slowly moved onto the path, following the cleric.

He placed his hand on the small of my back and gently nudged me forward. We all joined in and walked behind the string of coffins. We pulled our hoods and masks on, and the direct sunlight washed over us. My body felt warm, but my heart was heavy as I gazed forward at the dozens of lives lost, carried on the grieving shoulders of their brothers, their sisters, their mothers and fathers, while the rest of the city wept.

"There is no religion here," Caspian replied, "but there are traditions, which have been assigned to the cleric to help us remember and perform. We do not worship anyone or anything, but we honor life and grieve in death. Rituals help us fare better in loss."

The main road leading toward the base of the mountain was covered in black hooded beings, with wooden coffins stretching in a long line through the middle of the procession. Sunlight glistened on their lacquered surfaces. Birds trilled from trees nearby, almost matching the flutes playing at the front.

We reached the infirmary floor, where Scarlett and Patrik

awaited in their GASP uniforms, carrying Minah's coffin into the procession. They seamlessly blended in as we descended farther down the mountain. I glanced to the left and saw the daemon's body, wrapped up and burning on a funeral pyre built on the edge of the terrace outside the infirmary.

Rabid orange flames licked at the sky, consuming his flesh and spewing plumes of black smoke.

Several Correction Officers stood on the edge of the road, their heads and faces covered, their hands behind their backs. I could see their eyes through their smoky goggles—there was sadness in them, and anger, as they watched the procession.

Once we made our way down to the base of the mountain, we followed the flowery path all the way to the north side, where the cemetery awaited, several acres' worth of tombstones for the thousands of years of Azure Heights' existence. It looked strange but beautiful, with crypts nestled between trees with reddish foliage and white flowers sprinkled across the short, neatly trimmed grass. The caretaker in charge did a wonderful job of keeping the place up.

Rectangular holes had been dug and lined with white flowers. We all gathered around that portion of the cemetery. The Imen's caskets were lowered into the ground, and the cleric spoke of peace, of love, of the fragility and beauty of life, and of the hope that there is something there, beyond death. The people cried as they bid their farewells, stopping in front of each hole and dropping a flower inside.

Soon enough, the Imen's coffins were buried beneath flower

petals, with the cleric moving on to address the deceased Maras' families in his speech. The Maras' caskets were mounted on funeral pyres, surrounded by flowers, and were getting a different funeral service. The cleric walked between them, setting them alight with a small torch.

As the fires burned and crackled through the wood, the flames rising and black smoke billowing, Rewa stepped forward in front of her father's pyre, which had yet to be set on fire.

"We've all lost someone today," she said, her voice raw and trembling as she swallowed back tears. An Iman servant came to her side with an umbrella, so she could take off her mask and hood and reveal herself to the people. I assumed it was part of the tradition. "Whether you all knew the deceased or not, you have lost someone today. An Iman, a Mara, a brother... a sister, a father, a mother... a friend or a loved one... or just the neighbor you never speak to, or that person you bumped into the other day... You have all lost someone today. And I have lost someone, too..."

She choked up, and the cleric came by her side and gave her his flaming torch.

"I've lost my father," she continued, barely holding it together. "My best friend, my mentor... the only creature who has always understood and loved me unconditionally. Today, I burn the body of my father, Darius Xunn, Lord of Azure Heights. Today, we burn the body of our leader, our teacher, our protector and our fellow citizen. Tomorrow, the sun will rise again, and our world will be poorer without him, but far richer with the heritage he leaves behind..."

She took a deep breath, tears streaming down her cheeks, then turned around and set fire to her father's casket. The flames engulfed the funeral pyre, the wood crackling as the fire ate its way through it, turning everything to ashes.

I wasn't one to cry at funerals, but the atmosphere got to me —I realized that as I felt tears soaking into my mask. Caspian's hand took mine, and I gazed up at him. My eyesight was a little hazy with tears, but I managed to see the pained expression he wore as he looked at me. He gently squeezed my hand, a small but reassuring gesture that somehow meant the world to me.

As a sentry, I could see the sadness and frustration emanating from him in deep shades of blue and crimson. He had every reason to feel that way, and yet there was something more beneath those obvious layers. The golden tendrils I'd seen before, warm and almost palpable as they tickled my face. It was so strange and beautiful to experience, in the midst of all that grief.

Caspian had this effect on me, and I found that it didn't bother me. It didn't scare me, either. Sure, it confused the hell out of me, but his presence and his touch seemed to make it all worth it. He was an enigma I was determined to unravel, one layer at a time.

For the time being, however, I was thankful to have him standing next to me, holding my hand and filling my heart with an unfamiliar, peculiar, but wonderful kind of warmth.

As I lifted my goggles and wiped my tears, I glanced at Rewa for a minute. Her grief seemed genuine. Tears rolled down her pale cheeks and dripped into the short grass at her feet. Her head was down as the flutes and drums produced a mournful ballad to which they all knew the lyrics.

Her lips parted, then moved as she sang. Soon enough, the entire crowd joined in—a sea of voices singing about the ephemeral nature of life, about how a second and a thousand years are suddenly equal in the face of death.

It sent shivers down my spine, reminding me of how precious life was. Sure, I'd opted for immortality as a vampire. But that didn't mean it couldn't be taken away from me. It didn't mean that it wouldn't all come to an end at some point.

I instinctively squeezed Caspian's hand, then gave him a sideways glance as I wondered... If my life were to stop right here and now, I would never see him again. Something clawed at my heart in response, painful and unforgiving.

As our eyes met, I understood.

Caspian was slowly but surely becoming an extra reason for me to live and keep fighting.

13

———

CAIA

(DAUGHTER OF GRACE & LAWRENCE)

A luncheon was organized at the White Star Hotel, with a massive buffet covering the ground and first floor of the building, along with seating and more stalls on the front terrace, for all those who wished to join the grieving families of those lost in last night's attacks.

The banquet hall on the ground floor was enormous and beautifully decorated with floral spheres and black ribbons hanging from the domed ceiling. It was simple, but elegant and full of expression—an artful way of mourning, I thought.

Our team was given a table at the far end, secluded between large potted flowers that gave us a mild sense of privacy. Servants brought over pitchers of blood and mixed platters from the buffet. My gaze quietly followed them as they then took more blood pitchers to the Lords' table, on the opposite side of the hall.

The funeral ceremony had been quite intense and emotional, but something else bothered us, collectively. It hung heavy in the air between us, and it had to be addressed sooner rather than later.

"Why aren't they here yet?" I asked, and they all looked up at me. Their expressions told me everything I needed to know —I wasn't the only one thinking about it. "Seriously, it's been days now, and GASP isn't here yet. There's something wrong."

Jax took a long sip from his cup, then let out a long, exhausted sigh.

"I don't know, Caia," he replied, shaking his head slowly. "They should've been here by now, and frankly, I've been telling myself 'any minute now' for a couple of days... I do know that they would definitely try to come for us if they couldn't reach us via Telluris. Without a doubt, that I can guarantee you."

"But they're not here, so... what now?" I shrugged, crossing my arms over my chest. I lost my appetite, thinking about my parents, my sister, and everyone else who was waiting for us to come back safely. Worst of all, I was beginning to worry that maybe they'd already sent help, and something terrible might have happened along the way. Those were thoughts so terrible that I didn't want to voice them—voicing them would make them real.

"So, it's true, then. The asteroid belt is hindering GASP's access to Neraka," Fiona said, pouring herself a cup of spiced blood. "It isn't just stopping us from leaving; it's doing some-thing to outside forces, too?"

Several moments passed as we let the possibility really sink in. We'd already considered this earlier, but it still didn't make me feel any better. Nevertheless, it sounded reasonable enough to pass as a valid theory.

"It's already hindering communications, and it's keeping the planet hidden from the Daughters," Hansa mused, absently pushing steamed vegetables around her plate with a fork. "Maybe its effect was amplified over the past couple of days..."

"Disrupting interplanetary spells altogether?" Jax raised an eyebrow. "If that's true, then anyone who tried to pierce Neraka's atmosphere could very easily blow up in a ball of flames, too, like what Avril experienced—"

"But out of orbit," Avril interjected, her eyes wide with fear. "But wouldn't we have seen something in the sky, if that were the case?"

"Maybe... The interplanetary spell is quite accurate," Patrik said. "It brought us straight to Azure Heights. The Nerakian samples that Rewa left with Viola are from here, too. So it wouldn't be a question of an interplanetary spell landing on the wrong side of Neraka, for us not to see at all."

"What if it's cutting off magic altogether?" Fiona asked.

"That is possible," Patrik replied. "We'll definitely look into the asteroid belt while Jax and his team are out. There must be a way to disrupt its effect. Otherwise it would mean we're stuck here, with no way for GASP to reach us."

The idea fell heavily on all our shoulders. My stomach churned, and angst clawed its way up my throat. There was no way I'd be spending my life here. It was absurd, unacceptable, downright horrific.

Blaze's hand found mine under the table, and gave me a gentle squeeze.

"We'll find a way out, Caia," he said, his midnight-blue eyes settled on mine. "Even if I have to fly out there, as high as I can, and blow those things out of the sky..."

"I think that's physically impossible," I muttered, though grateful for his attempt to reassure me.

"Don't underestimate my abilities," he replied. "We are *not* staying here forever."

A couple of minutes went by in grim silence as we all looked at each other. I reached out for my glass of water but stilled as I noticed Vincent and Rewa approaching our table. Blaze didn't let go of my hand.

"Thank you all for attending the funeral today," Rewa said, her gaze settling on Blaze. "It meant a lot to me... to us."

"It was the least we could do, given everything that's happened," he replied softly.

"Yes... Well, in light of last night's event, I understand that you will head back to the gorges this afternoon." Rewa frowned, and Blaze nodded in response. "I suppose we'll have to postpone our dinner, then, until you return *safely* from your mission."

Even in mourning, Rewa was sweet on Blaze, judging by the

faint smile on her face. Had she not just cremated her father, I would've been a lot more annoyed, but, given the circumstances, all I could do was stop myself from rolling my eyes. Blaze squeezed my hand again, a secret gesture under the table that made me feel better.

"Thank you for understanding, Rewa," he replied.

My skin caught fire, not just from his touch but from the meaning of his gesture. Blaze knew how much I disliked Rewa's advances, and he was quite adamant about making it clear to me that he had no interest in her whatsoever. It made me want to wrap my arms around him and never let him go, but we were still at a funeral luncheon, and Rewa was still standing there, her gaze filled with sadness and longing as she smiled at Blaze.

"Fiona, I understand that you will be staying in the city with the rest of the team," Vincent said from where he stood next to her chair, his hands behind his back.

"That's right, we have a lot of work to do in the city, too," she replied with a nod.

"In that case, I was wondering if you would like to join me for dinner tonight. You've been through enough already, and I'd like to do something to lighten things up a little..."

Fiona's eyes grew wide, and she glanced around the table at us. She noticed my eyebrows rising with surprise, and she definitely registered Heron's mischievous grin, along with the nudge he got from Avril.

"It would be my pleasure," Fiona then replied, looking up at Vincent.

"Wonderful." He beamed at her. "I shall see you here at eight tonight, then. Thank you for accepting my invitation."

She gave him a soft smile, and he and Rewa excused themselves and returned to their table. Heron couldn't hold back anymore, chuckling as he poured himself a cup of blood.

"Even with a dead Lord and his sister gone to live with a daemon, Vincent does not stop pursuing you, Fi," Heron said. "The dude has the absolute hots for you!"

"I think it's your mouth that'll get you killed someday," Avril shot back, slapping him over the shoulder. He kept laughing, though, enough to infect us all and put smiles on our faces— even Avril's.

"Well, to be honest, I'm not interested in him, not like *that*, anyway," Fiona replied, staring at the blood in her cup. "But I do feel sorry for him, especially after what happened with Sienna. It's like... I just don't want to let him down. He's been through enough as it is."

"That's cute. He just said the same about you." Hansa smirked. "Do as you please, Fiona, but just be careful and stay safe at all times."

Fiona leaned into her chair and breathed out, her shoulders dropping slowly.

"I will. It's just dinner," she huffed.

I did understand where she was coming from. Based on what we'd seen so far, Vincent liked her a lot, but he was also a gentleman who tried to do right by everyone. He'd been in the gorges with us, he'd seen the dangers we faced, and he'd later seen the real damage that the daemons could do to his people, far beyond the abductions.

But he couldn't deny the fact that he liked Fiona. It was so endearingly obvious by the way he longingly gazed at her whenever he was around. Even now, as he resumed his seat at the Lords' table, Vincent glanced over his shoulder and across the hall, just to get a glimpse of Fiona.

Blaze's hand was still clutching mine, I realized. I turned my head and found him quietly studying me. There was a look in his eyes that I couldn't quite comprehend, but it made my spine tingle and my temperature rise by a few degrees.

We were going back to the Valley of Screams. And I was determined to make sure that we all came back in one piece and with crucial information about our enemies. I dreaded the thought of going underground after the daemons, but, at the same time, I found comfort in the fact that Blaze was coming with us.

You don't bring a lighter into daemon city. You bring a dragon.

14

AVRIL

(DAUGHTER OF LUCAS & MARION)

After the funeral luncheon, we gathered back outside the infirmary, which had basically become our little HQ. Harper, Jax, Hansa, Blaze, and Caia stopped by the Broken Bow Inn first, to gear up and pack some additional supplies.

Caspian soon joined us, his servants bringing down indigo horses. Jax then handed Patrik a small box with various objects belonging to the group.

"We estimate at least a day and a half for this, "Jax said. "To find a daemon and make our way into a daemon city. If we're not back by midnight tomorrow, use the items in this box for a tracking spell to find us."

"We'll do that." Patrik nodded firmly. "Scarlett and I will check the city's library in full, top to bottom, to get as much information as possible on the asteroid belt."

"And Fiona, Heron, and I will look for Cynara and her sister," I said. "Hopefully we'll be able to shed some light on the treatment of Imen in this city, at least until we see Arrah again and she gives us the whole scoop."

"We'd also like your permission to use some of the invisibility spell ingredients for another prison inspection," Heron added, looking at Jax. "I don't think we're done with that place just yet."

Jax thought about it for a few seconds, then nodded.

"Do whatever you think will help this investigation, Heron," he replied, "but make sure you prioritize. We'll bring back some invisibility spell samples from the daemons, for Patrik to break down into ingredients, so we can replenish our own supply."

"It dawned on me, by the way, why the daemons' invisibility spell is different, in that you catch a glimpse of the air rippling and the red eyes... plus the water issue," Patrik interjected, "and I've given it some thought. It makes sense. The original invisibility spell uses specific ingredients, some of which I don't think exist on Neraka, though I'll check their biology books, just in case. So, they must have found local ingredients to use, which change the behavior of the spell altogether."

It sank in then. Patrik had a point. The daemons had taken a swamp witch spell and had adapted it to their environment. The same must have happened with the other charms in their possession.

"They're devious bastards, aren't they?" I frowned and shook my head slowly, my loathing of their entire species burning at the back of my throat.

"It makes sense," Jax agreed. "Then we'll definitely bring back samples."

We bid our farewells and watched as Jax, Hansa, Caspian, Harper, Blaze, and Caia got on their indigo horses and left for the gorges. They darted down the main road and became small black dots crossing the two-mile plain separating the mountain from the Valley of Screams.

"Okay, we'll head to the library next," Scarlett said as Patrik moved closer to her.

"And we'll go up to the South Bend Inn to find Cynara and Hera." I nodded. "Surely they'll have something interesting to tell us."

"Let's meet back here at midnight tonight," Patrik replied.

We had half an afternoon and an entire evening left to cover as much ground as possible. Heron, Fiona, and I had agreed to use up some of the invisibility spell supply for the prison, just to get a better look at the prisoners. It was odd that they'd all been mind-bent, and we needed to ascertain the extent of their mental manipulation.

But first, we needed to check in on Cynara. The first night we met, just after our arrival, Cynara had acted strangely toward us. There was a fear in her eyes, an uneasiness that didn't make sense. Hera's explanation about losing family members in the abduction didn't make me less suspicious, and Heron and Fiona weren't buying it, either.

Even with the attack, the funeral, and the grief that had stricken the city, I'd yet to lose my doubts about the Maras' treatment of Imen. Whether it was something innocent or downright nefarious, we needed to know.

Diplomacy or not, if the Imen were being abused in any way, on top of what was already happening with the daemons, I was going to raise hell in Azure Heights.

15

AVRIL

(DAUGHTER OF LUCAS & MARION)

Heron used his mind-bending to persuade the Iman girl in charge of the South Bend Inn's reception to tell us which room Cynara and Hera were in. We knocked on the door and were greeted by a baffled Cynara, her eyes puffy and tears still drying on her rosy cheeks.

"Hi, Cynara, I'm not sure you remember us," I said, smiling gently. "I'm Avril, and this is Heron and Fiona."

"Yes, I... I remember," Cynara murmured. She frowned and avoided looking at us directly. I caught a glimpse of her sister behind her. "You were the Lords' guests for dinner at the Broken Bow Inn."

"And you're here to help us," Hera interjected, joining her sister's side.

"That's right," I replied. "We're trying to prevent last night from happening again, among other things. We're all so sorry for your losses…"

Hera pushed the door open with a brief nod, but Cynara didn't look happy about it. Somehow, the roles had changed. Last time, Hera had been the secretive one, protecting her sister and removing her from the situation. In all fairness, the Lords *were* watching during that dinner.

"Come in," Hera said, and cleared the way for us. Cynara kept herself behind Hera, a concerned expression pulling her eyebrows closer.

We went inside, and Hera closed the door and locked it.

A couple of minutes went by in silence. I looked at Heron. He gave me a confident wink—he wanted to take control of the conversation. Hera and Cynara stayed close to each other, keeping some distance from us.

"We were wondering if you could tell us more about the Imen people," Heron started, while Fiona and I glanced around the room.

There wasn't much there that belonged to the girls. They'd probably lost everything in the attack. I noticed clothes on a chair and some toiletries on a dresser, but other than that, the room carried the neutral aspect of a guesthouse.

"What would you like to know?" Hera replied.

"How many Imen live outside the city?" Heron asked, his hands behind his back as he assumed a non-threatening posture. I figured he didn't want to try mind-bending and was looking to see how much they could tell us on their own.

"To be honest, we're not very sure." Hera shrugged, while Cynara pulled a chair from the side and took a seat next to her. She seemed worn out, the sadness in her eyes rubbing off on me. "Our people separated thousands of years ago. We haven't really stayed in touch with the Imen beyond the Valley of Screams."

"Are there any records of them? The library didn't have anything," Heron said.

Hera and Cynara looked at each other, slightly surprised.

"Well, some of the elder Imen in the city keep archives, but nobody knows about them, especially not the Maras." Hera nodded. "It's a secret. Only a handful of us are aware, for that matter."

"You managed to keep it a secret from the Maras? Why is that?" I asked.

"I... I don't know exactly," Hera replied. "I just know we have to keep it from them."

Heron then looked at me, his lips pressed into a thin line.

"They've been mind-bent," he said. "But the Maras never got to clear their memories about the Imen's archives, because they had no knowledge of them existing in the first place. Call it a loophole."

"I do have gaps in my memory." Hera sighed, resting a hand on her sister's shoulder. Cynara's eyes were getting droopy—yet another sign of emotional and physical exhaustion. "There are things I don't remember, but I should. And there are things I know happened, but don't have a single image in my head to match them to. It's like I know of certain events... but I can't actually remember them. Is that also mind-bending?"

"It is." Heron nodded. "And it confirms what I've suspected since we first got here. The Maras have been systematically wiping your memories, replacing ideas and facts in your heads... to fit a specific narrative, I suppose."

"But why would they do that?" Hera shrugged. "We've been staying here voluntarily, living and working with them. Why would they mind-bend us?"

A moment passed as we thought about possible reasons. Fiona moved farther to the back, leaning against the window frame and crossing her arms over her chest.

"Are you sure you've stayed here voluntarily?" she asked, looking at Hera and Cynara. "What do you remember about it?"

"Just what we've always been taught," Hera replied. "From the day we were born, we've been told that the Imen and Exiled Maras live in peace. We coexist and support each other, and Azure Heights is our home."

"Do you remember your parents telling you that, specifically?" Heron narrowed his eyes, carefully analyzing the Imen girls' expressions. They stared blankly ahead, then at each other as the unpleasant truth set in.

"No..." Cynara breathed, then gave us a frightened look. "Does... Does this mean they've mind-bent us into believing that?"

"Most likely, yes." Heron sighed. "But I suggest you put that thought away for the time being, at least until we figure out what's going on here. It isn't safe for you to question anything that the Maras tell you at this point."

The girls lowered their heads, their hands resting in their laps. They seemed genuinely distraught, and I couldn't really blame them for feeling that way. After all, their whole lives could very well be blatant lies, and they had no control over their own minds. Their memories were incomplete, and some, if not most, weren't even theirs to begin with.

"I don't know how we can do that." Hera shuddered. "I'm mad... I am so angry right now... I feel so helpless."

"And the Maras... They seem to know everything," Cynara added. "I don't think we can pretend."

"What if I mind-bend you into forgetting we were ever here tonight?" Heron offered, and both Fiona and I frowned at him.

"Have they not been through enough of that?" Fiona replied.

"Well, it's the only way for them to pass as mind-bent." Heron shrugged. "As Maras, we are capable of detecting changes in a creature's behavior, and right now, I can tell you that both Hera's and Cynara's heartrates have increased. They cannot lie to me, and they certainly won't be able to lie to the others. If I clear their memories of this meeting altogether, they will have nothing to lie about."

"He's right," Hera said, though she clearly disliked the prospect of another memory wipe. "Especially since we've told you about the archives. We cannot risk it. Do it."

"Look for old Iman Lemuel," Cynara added. "He lives on the

third level; he has a small bookstore on the ground floor of his house. He's well known to the people there, so you won't have trouble finding his place. We know he has some ancient texts hidden somewhere in there."

"But try visiting him in the morning, as he's usually out during the day, and leaves his niece in charge of the library. I don't think she knows about the archives," Hera replied. "He likes to paint, and is always out and about, looking for the perfect landscape..."

"Thank you both." Heron gave them a warm smile, then stepped forward, and I could see his eyes flickering gold as he mind-bent them. "You won't remember us coming here. You won't remember talking to us, nor will you remember the fact that you know you're being mind-bent. My friends and I will walk out of here, and, shortly afterward, you will forget this meeting ever happened."

The sisters nodded slowly, their pupils dilating and their expressions attaining an eerie kind of serenity, as Heron motioned for us to leave. We reached the corridor and closed the door behind us.

"I really hope they don't get into any trouble because of us," I murmured as we went down the stairs and left the inn behind.

"Chances are slim to none," Heron replied. "They won't remember anything, so there's nothing for them to be aware or afraid of. They'll be okay."

Fiona stepped in front of us, bringing Heron and me to a halt.

"Let's be smart about this," she said, pursing her lips. "Let's get to Lemuel's bookstore first. Avril, you can pick up his scent from there, then take Heron with you and track the old Iman to wherever he is. There's no point in waiting until morning."

"I agree." I nodded. "Time is of the essence here."

"Besides, that way we handle Lemuel, and you get to do your fancy dinner with Vincent." Heron grinned, and I playfully smacked him on the shoulder.

My reaction made him chuckle, and Fiona gave us a half-smile in return. She wasn't in the best of moods, but, given everything that had happened, I wasn't sure what to blame it on.

"You okay, Fi?" I asked softly.

"Yes, mostly," she said. "I'm just getting more worried about the whole mind-bending thing. We've been so busy with the daemons and then the explosion that we haven't had much time to properly look into this. I guess Heron and Jax were right that we can't fully trust the Exiled Maras."

"Honestly, I wish I was wrong," Heron muttered, glancing over his shoulder at the inn. Lights were flickering in the windows as the evening set in, casting shades of purple and violet across the sky. "I wish they were all innocent and all we had to worry about was daemons, but... turns out we're not that lucky."

Indeed, we weren't lucky at all. We'd already suspected that there was something off about the relationship between the Exiled Maras and the Imen, but only now were we finally beginning to peel away the layers of secrets over this picture-perfect city.

It wasn't perfect at all. Imen's minds had been repeatedly erased. Memories had been replaced with false knowledge. There was something terribly off in this city, far beyond the daemons' recent targeting of its people.

And we were going to get to the bottom of it, one way or another.

16

HARPER

(DAUGHTER OF HAZEL & TEJUS)

We raced across the plains, our indigo horses ridiculously swift, as always. The tall grass and cloudy skies allowed us to blend in a little better as we passed through small bundles of trees to avoid making a straight, clear line.

The idea was that daemons could be watching from the gorges, and they could potentially see us coming in. If we made the most of our surroundings and the trees nearby, we could avoid detection. We reached a cluster of rocks just five hundred yards away from the stream leading into the Valley of Screams, and Jax urged us to stop.

We pulled our horses into the shade as the sun set behind the limestone giants ahead, turning the sky purple with streaks of white clouds gathering. The air felt more humid than usual, signaling potential rain.

"If it rains, it'll work in our favor," Jax said as he pulled out the map, spreading it against the vertical wall of one of the rocks. "It'll wash over our tracks, making it harder for daemons to track us."

I looked around, using my True Sight to detect any enemy activity, but all I could see were wild animals grazing through green patches in the nearby gorges. Jax analyzed the map carefully as we gathered around him.

"What are you thinking?" Hansa asked, squinting at the sinuous lines of each ravine.

"I don't think it's wise if we take one of the central routes through the gorges this time," Jax replied, pointing at the stream line. "We're doing recon and don't want to be detected at all, so I was thinking we could try one of the less traveled paths. What are your thoughts, Caspian?"

"I couldn't agree more," Caspian replied from my side, then placed his index finger on a gorge closer to the ocean side, about one mile to the south from our position. "This could be a good entry point. It's somewhat secluded, and narrow enough for us to make good use of crevices to hide in, in case daemons come along. We could set a trap here, three hundred yards away from the pond. The area is dense with trees, and there's a clearing in this spot that could help with laying the trap."

I looked up at him, quietly fascinated by his profile—the blade of his nose and deep-set jade eyes creating an extremely attractive ensemble with his lips and slightly sharp chin. He gave me a brief sideways glance and caught me staring. I immediately shifted my focus to the map, holding my breath. I knew his eyes were still on me.

"That sounds like a good plan." Jax nodded, then rolled the map up and stuffed it into his backpack.

We got back onto our horses and rushed over to the south side, where the narrowest of the gorges awaited. Caspian was right—the ravine was stuffed with large trees and shrubs, perfect for us to move through without being detected.

I stayed at the front as we entered the Valley of Screams, with Caspian by my side. Jax and Hansa stayed behind us, followed by Caia and Blaze. I briefly scanned the area and noticed a cave opening about fifty feet away in the right wall. The wind whispered past our ears, carrying with it the promise of darkness and rain. Birds chirped from the tree crowns stretching overhead, and I caught glimpses of deer and boarlike animals shuffling across the path ahead.

"There's a cave there." I pointed toward the west. "We can use it for the horses."

We reached it in a matter of minutes, our mounts trotting cautiously as we inspected every inch around us. I wouldn't be able to see the daemons, but I could capture movement in branches and shrubs whenever it happened and trace it back to a wild animal. If there was nothing to trace it back to, it would mean we had company.

For the time being, however, we were okay. We got off the

horses, and I guided them into the cave, while the others watched. I took hold of Caspian's horse and looked into its beautiful, sapphire-blue eyes.

"All of you stay here," I said softly, stroking its neck. "Do not flee unless you're under attack. Stay hidden, out of sight. Protect the others. Only come out if the coast is clear, and if you need to feed. We'll be back soon."

The stallion neighed and shook its head in response, then nuzzled my face with a huff, making me giggle.

"I have to say, I don't think I'll ever get tired of watching you do that," Caspian said. I turned around and found him gazing admiringly at me.

"Thank you... I guess," I murmured with a modest shrug.

"Okay, let's move forward now," Jax said, and we continued on foot.

Not ten minutes later, we came across a creepy but good sign that we were in the right place. Imen skeletons were scattered between the tall pine-like trees, the bones cleaned and yellowed by the passage of time.

My stomach tightened as I got closer to one, realizing that I was looking at what had once been the body of a teenage Iman girl, judging by the shape of the hip bones and the locks of brown hair beneath the skull.

"There are definitely daemons in these parts," Jax muttered as he stared at another set of bones. Strips of clothing were still wrapped around parts of the skeletons, and moss had grown on the sides of their skulls.

"They've been here for years." Caspian frowned. "No one bothered to take them away, or bury them. Judging by their clothes, they don't belong to the same group or tribe. My guess is that this is a feeding ground for hunter daemons without caves."

"So there will be some lurking around, you think?" I asked, then shuddered as a chill ran down my spine. I moved closer to the middle of the road, and closer to Caspian, who nodded.

"We'll need to move forward a little and get to the clearing I showed you. We can lay a trap there, but we'll need bait. An open wound, something to spark their interest. They are drawn to the scent of blood, in general, like any other predator," he said.

Several moments passed as we looked at each other, until Hansa slowly raised her hand.

"I'll be the damsel in distress," she said with a smirk, making both Caia and me chuckle.

"Oh, please, you're neither a damsel, nor ever in actual distress," I replied.

"You're a freaking warrior," Caia added.

"Come on, I can do it," Hansa shot back, amusement flickering in her emerald-gold eyes.

"I don't think that's a good idea." Jax frowned, crossing his arms over his chest.

Hansa rolled her eyes, then slowly shook her head and stared ahead.

"You keep underestimating me, Jaxxon Dorchadas," she

retorted. "How much more will it take for you to understand that I'm not someone you can try to 'protect'?"

"I'm only expressing concern for—"

"Don't," she interrupted Jax. "I'm perfectly capable of acting as bait, and you know it."

Something strange happened—something I'd never seen before. Jax didn't fight her on this any longer. His shoulders dropped as he conceded, his gaze fixed on her. The dynamic between them had changed. It was all there, particularly in the way they looked at each other. There was muted affection and a sliver of resentment.

"Okay, it's settled then," I replied. "Hansa will be the most unconvincing bait we've ever had, and that's it."

I walked toward the clearing, followed by the rest of our team. Caspian kept himself close to me, and I occasionally stole glances at him as we moved between the trees. The sky darkened above as evening gradually descended upon us with cool winds, nocturnal insects buzzing all around.

"How are you faring after last night?" I asked him after a couple of minutes.

"I'll be fine," he replied, keeping his eyes on the path ahead. "Half of my household died in the explosions, but there is no time to mourn. All I can do is keep pushing and help you bring those responsible to justice."

"I'm... I'm truly sorry," I murmured, an invisible string tugging at my heart. "Were they friends, family?"

"They were both," he sighed. "Some were cousins of mine,

but most were servants. They'd been with my House for years. Few people know what it's like inside House Kifo, but one thing I can guarantee is that no one wants for anything in my house. I look after my own, and their extended families. They're irreplaceable, and we'll all have to learn to live without them. But we *will* live. No matter what."

I nodded slowly, but there was something in the way he spoke that made me think there was an underlying statement there. Caspian was so full of secrets, I had a hard time *not* picking up on the details he slipped into his every sentence. He was trying to tell me more about himself and his world without actually saying anything. That had to be quite the feat, and I knew by that point that he would eventually open up to me.

His aura was a mixture of gold and green whenever he was close to me, and, while I'd yet to figure out exactly what that meant, it felt positive and... nice. The looks he gave me were different, too. There was warmth in the jade pools of his eyes. The tension between us was gradually subsiding, replaced by something else—a thickness in the air that I wasn't sure how to interpret, for the time being. Caspian was a creature who required some patience to fully understand; that was the one thing I was absolutely certain about.

And I had already decided that I would take my time and let him come to me. He wanted to share his secrets, and I'd made it my mission to earn his full trust for this. It turned out that Jax and Hansa weren't the only ones whose dynamic had changed...

17

HARPER

(DAUGHTER OF HAZEL & TEJUS)

About an hour later, we'd all assumed our positions in hidden parts of the clearing. Hansa was out in the open, sitting in the very middle of the path with a self-inflicted cut on her thigh. Silvery blood dripped from it, gathering in the dust beneath, as she leaned onto her hands and waited. She was getting bored, occasionally clicking her teeth just to break through the silence.

We'd used ropes and trees nearby to set some snare traps. There was a wide circle around Hansa, buried in the dirt, ready to snap as soon as a daemon caught the scent of her blood and got close enough for Jax to pull and release the trap.

Caspian and I were hidden behind a slab of limestone just forty feet away, with our backs against the stone and one of the snare ropes in my hands, waiting for a daemon to come by. My

True Sight was constantly on, and I looked around, expecting to see the air rippling sooner or later.

Blaze, Caia, and Jax were somewhere on the other side of the path, holding onto their own lengths of rope. Half an hour had gone by with no sign of hostiles. We knew it was going to be a waiting game, though.

Caspian was standing so close to me that I could smell his fragrance of choice—a nose-tingling mixture of musk and spices that made my stomach tighten with delight. I casually looked up and found his gaze on my face, intense and cloudy. He lowered his head so slowly that I barely registered the movement until I realized that our lips were mere inches apart.

I held my breath. Time stopped as we looked into each other's eyes, and waves of gold emanated from him, subtle shades that persisted in my field of vision. My heart thundered almost painfully with anticipation, until my senses came back into focus. Raindrops started falling, almost instantly evaporating as they hit my face.

Caspian blinked several times and seemed to regain his composure. *What is going on here? What... What is this between us?*

"I thought about that one question," I whispered, trying to steer myself back into reality. Hansa was still out there in the middle of the path, and I needed to stay sharp. Caspian seemed to smile with just his eyes as he waited patiently for me to continue. "Have you ever spoken to daemons? Do you know any daemons, and have you ever been to their underground cities?"

"That's more than one question." He smirked.

"They pertain to the same topic." I rolled my eyes. "Come on, man, after all we've been through, I deserve some answers! We all do!"

He thought about it for a couple of seconds, then let out a muted groan in surrender. "Yes, I've spoken to daemons."

I froze, the entire picture of him suddenly revealed anew, now brighter, more nuanced, at such a revelation. He looked away, and I registered the change in his expression: his gaze darkened, and his eyebrows pulled closer together.

"Yes, I know plenty of daemons," he breathed. "And yes, I've been underground, too. It's why I suggested this side of the gorge in the first place. There's an access tunnel not far from here, but it's hidden with a cloaking spell, and we'll need a live daemon to open it."

"That means... Wait, cloaking spell," I murmured, putting two and two together. "Swamp witch magic, right?"

He nodded.

"They're very resourceful," he muttered, his disdain obvious. At least I knew he didn't have a good relationship with the daemons...

"The original cloaking spell requires the blood of someone who was in the protected space when the magic was first cast," I remembered. "In this case, however, assuming it has to do with using slightly different ingredients from Neraka, it needs a live specimen. Correct?"

"That's right. Hence why I thought laying a trap was a good

idea," he replied, the corner of his mouth twitching. "You and your team continue to surprise me in a most positive way."

Something heavy weighed on my chest as I stared at him, a mixture of frustration and... well, attraction swirling through me. I liked Caspian. A lot. More than I'd originally thought possible, but he was so secretive at a time when any sliver of information could make the difference between life and death. I was conflicted.

"I can't help but wonder if you'll ever share your secrets with us. With me." I let out a long, tortured sigh, just to relieve some of the tension gathering inside my ribcage. "I honestly think you'll be the end of me and my team if you keep hiding these things from us..."

My burst of honesty was inevitable. I'd known I'd cave in at some point and just voice my thoughts to him, and I actually felt a little better after I let it all out. But Caspian continued to surprise me. He gripped my chin with his thumb and index finger, and turned my head for me to face him.

"I won't let anything happen to you *or* your team, Miss Hell-swan, I promise you," he said softly, and my limbs tingled at the sound of his raspy voice, his breath warming my face. "It's why I am here, with you. I've been trying to stop you from walking into a disaster from the day you arrived on Neraka, but, since clearly I can't get you to leave this place, I will do my best to keep you all alive. Although, technically speaking, as of last night it seems that Neraka doesn't want you to leave, anyway..."

We stayed like that for a while—it seemed like forever. I

allowed myself to sink my consciousness into the deep jade green of his eyes. For a moment, the whole world disappeared as we looked at each other, while I tried to figure out what it was that sparked such wildfires between us.

"I can't come forward with *everything* I know, not yet, anyway," he continued. My whole body felt warm, and I feared his proximity might become addictive. "There are still pieces of my plan that I need to put in place, pieces that require more time on my end. But I assure you, as soon as everything is where I need it to be... as soon as I secure the safety of those innocent of any crime, I will tell you the truth. All of it."

It was the most I would get from Caspian, for the time being. It was better than nothing, and it confirmed what I'd already been suspecting. He was protecting someone with his secrecy—more than one person, in fact. He'd said it before, but it was starting to sink in now.

18

HANSA

More than half an hour had passed since I'd plopped myself down in the middle of the clearing and cut a six-inch gash across my left thigh to draw out a hunter daemon. It was getting dark, and my boredom was starting to set in. The mild rain hadn't helped either, as water had soaked into my hair, making my head feel heavy. On top of that, water removed the daemons' invisibility spell, so, if they were going to attack me, they had to wait it out. Fortunately, it had stopped raining for the last ten minutes. I let out an occasional moan of pain, looking around to catch signs of any movement. But nothing happened.

I stretched my arms out and glanced to my left. Jax was beneath the thick crown of a bent tree, quietly watching me with a rope in his hand. We hadn't spoken about the kiss, and I felt a little disheartened—not because of him, but mostly because of how the universe had stopped us from talking about it, first by nearly killing Avril and then by blowing up the top level of the mountain and killing dozens of Maras and Imen.

Nevertheless, something had changed between us. I could tell from the way he looked at me. There was a more permanent softness lingering in his jade eyes whenever he did so—a softness that wasn't there before. I wondered if he would finally get over whatever insecurities were hounding him, and come to me. I'd made it clear that I was waiting, so the ball was basically in his court. The waiting game was a pain, though...

I picked up a handful of pebbles and started tossing them around, moaning louder—but with less conviction. It felt like I was dragging it out, but I figured making some noise might get the attention of one of the horned bastards lurking nearby.

"Somebody help me... Please... I'm in so much pain!" I cried out.

Jax raised an eyebrow at me, and I gave him a shrug in response.

Hey, whatever works, buddy!

One of my pebbles hit something in the air, twenty feet away from me. I stilled, watching the invisible form ripple closer, moving toward me. I cleared my throat, then gave Jax a sideways glance. He nodded briefly and waited for the daemon to get inside the snare trap hidden in the dirt.

I caught a glimpse of the fiend's glimmering red eyes.

"Oh no," I said, my tone much too flat. "Please don't hurt me..."

It stepped inside the snare trap, and I immediately pushed myself back and out of its range. Blaze, Jax, and Harper pulled the strings back, and—snap! We got him, the ropes tightening around his large form as he struggled against their hold.

Caia came out and tossed water from her flask, revealing the daemon in his full, savage splendor. Jax flashed behind him and brought his knife up to his throat, the white blade digging into his tanned skin and drawing a droplet of blood.

"Got you," Jax breathed. The daemon stilled, cursing under his breath.

Blaze and Harper came out, along with Caspian, and used the lengths of their ropes to further restrict the fiend's movements. They tied his hands behind his back, wrapping the rope tightly around his wrists.

"Make sure you really tighten those wrist bindings," Caspian told Harper. "You don't want him to bend his palms for his claws to reach the rope. It'll cut off his blood circulation, but you really shouldn't care about that."

"You're all going to die," the daemon hissed.

"I'd be more worried about yourself, if I were you," I shot back with a grin.

"Duly noted." Harper smirked and jerked the rope even tighter, prompting the daemon to grunt from the pain. She measured him from head to toe, and frowned slightly. "He's not as big as the others."

"No, he isn't." Caspian nodded.

"I can still slit your throats!" the daemon growled,

prompting Caspian to give him a hard backhand in response. His head jerked to the right, and he groaned from the pain, his lower lip split. He then opened his mouth, letting out a cricket-like sound, quickly muffled by Caspian, who tied a long piece of torn fabric over his mouth.

"You're not calling for help," the Mara said, then glanced at us, while I sized the daemon up for a brief moment.

Harper was right. The daemon was some inches shorter than Tobiah, and his muscle mass was substantially reduced, too. I had a feeling he was a weaker specimen.

"The lower-rank hunters, the weaker ones, that is, hunt on the outskirts of the Valley of Screams. The bigger and stronger they are, the easier their access to the main gorges, where most of their victims travel," Caspian explained.

Called it.

And then it hit me.

"Damn it, Lord Kifo, you could've said something sooner." I scoffed. "Preferably before we dragged our asses through the main gorge yesterday!"

"I agree, and I do apologize for that." Caspian nodded, grabbing the daemon's chin to get a better look at his face. "However, you were following a tracking spell yesterday. I don't think a side road would've made any difference. But I will be more than happy to make it up to you all, and take you to an access point leading to the underground. This fellow here will help us get through."

That didn't sound right. I'd thought we were going to

compel the daemon to show us the entrance to his city. It turned out that Caspian had known all along where to go. I crossed my arms over my chest and scowled at him, just to get my point across. The Mara gave me an apologetic shrug.

"Care to explain, Lord Kifo?" Jax frowned as he took hold of the daemon, who watched our exchange with a flicker of amusement in his red eyes.

"There's an access point not far from here," Caspian explained briefly. "It's cloaked with swamp witch magic, and it requires a live daemon for us to go through and reach the underground city. It's why I suggested coming through here in the first place."

Several seconds went by as we all stared at Caspian—Harper was the only one who didn't seem surprised. She noticed my curious expression and gave me an apologetic shrug of her own, as if mirroring Caspian's gestures. Those two were sort of made for each other.

"He told me just now," she murmured, looking like a kid caught with her hand in the honey jar.

Yeah, two peas from different worlds, fitting perfectly in the same pod, and they don't even know it. To be fair, I'd noticed the stolen glances already. I saw how they looked at each other, even when *they* weren't paying attention. There was something brewing between them—it had looked like quite the storm in the beginning, but Caspian had softened considerably since last night.

Oh, wow. I understood then how similar Caspian and Jax

were. They'd both adopted these big, gentle eyes whenever they saw us...

"I just wanted to see how capable you all are," Caspian said, breaking my train of thought. Blaze finished tying the rest of the rope around the daemon's torso, holding his arms in place. "You're all quite adept at killing *and* ensnaring daemons; hence, I am now comfortable with sharing more information. Don't take it personally. It's self-preservation that leads me to make such decisions. But rest assured, GASP continues to surprise me in a very positive way, and I never saw it coming."

I exhaled sharply and took out a healing pellet from the first-aid satchel mounted on my belt. I popped it into my mouth and chewed, then swallowed the herbal mixture, allowing it to dissolve inside my stomach. It was quickly absorbed into my bloodstream, and I felt my thigh wound tingling as it closed up.

Blessed be that Druid magic!

"Okay then, let's go," I replied, hands on my hips, as droplets of water came down from the sky once more. "Chop-chop! It's raining again!"

Caspian nodded and walked forward down the path. I could hear the rain rapping the surface of the pond just fifty yards away. The sky was dark above us, charcoal clouds keeping the first moon hidden. It worked to our advantage, as we could use the obscurity of trees and stones in this narrow ravine to get to where we needed with minimum exposure to daemon attacks.

Blaze and Jax grabbed the daemon and forced him to follow us, while Caia stayed by their side and Harper moved to the front so she could walk alongside Caspian. Yes, there was definitely something happening between them, and my protective instinct was ringing all sorts of alarm bells.

I decided to keep an eye on them. Not that I disliked Caspian, but given all the secrecy, I had a hard time fully trusting him and an even harder time letting Harper get too close to him. I just didn't want her to get hurt in *any* way.

There are few things in this world that are more painful than a heartbreak. One of them is the loss of a child.

And I had experienced both, repeatedly.

No way I'm letting her go through any of it...

19

HARPER

(DAUGHTER OF HAZEL & TEJUS)

Caspian led the way up the ravine, then through a couple of narrow passages that took us to another gorge. I stayed by his side, followed closely by Hansa and Caia, while Jax and Blaze held the daemon at the back.

The rain had stopped, and the ground was mushy beneath us, slathering our boots in mud as we snuck deeper into the Valley of Screams. Two hours passed as we occasionally hid behind large rocks and in tight crevices—I'd become quite adept at noticing the air ripple across larger distances with my True Sight, to the point where I could detect daemon movement before they got close enough to spot us.

"It's here," Caspian whispered as we made a sharp turn to the left upon exiting the third passage. The gorge stretching both ways was quite narrow and barren, riddled with sharp stones and yellow-colored shrubs.

There was a cave opening in the limestone wall on our left, not easy to spot with all the boulders partially blocking the entrance. From certain angles, one could pass by and not even notice it. We followed Caspian inside, moving through a dark tunnel that went on for about three hundred yards before it hit a... dead end.

"Are you sure we're on the right path?" I muttered, frowning at the sight of the stone wall.

"Look beyond." He gave me a sideways glance, the corner of his mouth twitching. I used my True Sight, and, what do you know, the tunnel kept going at a lower angle, deep underground.

"Okay, what now?" I raised my eyebrows. Caspian nodded at our daemon.

"Bring that sack of meat over here," he replied bluntly, and I let out a brief chuckle.

"Ooh, didn't know you had that sass in you!" I quipped, and he responded with a slyly raised eyebrow before taking hold of the daemon, who was still squirming and growling against his restraints.

Caspian took a small knife out of his belt and cut across the daemon's shoulder, drawing blood. The fiend hissed, and found himself pushed into the wall. The cloaking spell instantly reacted, and the limestone surface rippled.

"After you." Caspian smirked and bowed curtly.

I grinned as I stepped through the wall, the cool stone tickling my face with liquid motion. The rest of my team followed, dragging the daemon along with them. Caspian then grabbed the fiend and pushed him into a corner, slitting his throat with one swift move.

I gasped. He held the daemon in place, pressing a forearm into his chest as blood gushed from the gash across his throat. The creature gurgled and choked until the light in his eyes went out. Caspian pulled himself back, and the daemon slumped on the floor behind a couple of rocks.

"We couldn't risk him getting loose, and we don't need him down there," Caspian said, noticing my furrowed brow.

"No, it's fine. It makes sense." I shrugged. There was no issue with Caspian killing a daemon—even though this one had been restrained and could not harm us in any way. I was just surprised by the speed with which he made that decision, and the swiftness with which he executed it. Caspian had the cold blood of a killer if needed, and I knew it was in the best interest of our group.

"Let's go," he breathed, and went ahead.

One by one we descended after him. The tunnel got narrower every hundred yards, until we had to crouch in order to pass through it. Once we reached the exit, we followed him across a small plateau and hid behind the large rocks on the edge. It was secluded enough to keep us concealed as we took in our surroundings.

I held my breath as I looked up—a massive dome ceiling

stretched for tens of square miles, with thick pillars pouring down into the city to support its titanic weight. The daemon city below sprawled across the cave floor—riddled with square houses and buildings, made entirely out of black stone with obsidian reflexes. Orange fires burned in massive copper bowls at street junctions and in iron and glass boxes mounted on almost every wall.

The sight before me resembled a painting of a Renaissance inferno I'd seen in a museum back on Earth, with deep and dramatic contrasts of black and amber, of light and dark, and of sharp and soft forms in a terrifying display of what could easily be described as hell. Slim, pointy towers poked out from the sea of buildings, and thin streams of freaking lava poured through the city, crossed by a multitude of bridges.

It was hot all over, like a midsummer's day, dry enough to make me lick my lips every other minute because I was suddenly feeling all crusty and about to crumble. The center of the city was rich in immense buildings with tall columns and foundations, the latter linked to the black stone pavement through broad stairs. Farther outward, the buildings began to shrink, while the outskirts were occupied by small houses and modest huts.

Thousands of daemons roamed through the streets, and even they varied in size depending on their proximity to the city center. The rich, big, and strong ones lived in the middle of this massive settlement, while the weaklings were cast off to the sides.

Survival of the fittest, I guess...

"Keep your heads down," Caspian hissed, and pulled me back under the shade of our rocky cover. We all huddled closer together.

My heart stopped, and ice tumbled through my veins at the sound of a gut-wrenching shriek. I looked up and saw giant black bat-like creatures flying overhead. There were three of them, gliding in tandem as they took a tight turn and resumed their survey of the city.

"Those are Death Claws," Caspian breathed, watching them fly away.

They were scary as hell, with long, skinny legs and large wings that also served as arms. Each wing ended in a large claw, which explained why they were called Death Claws—those things were just a fraction of Blaze's dragon size, but they looked perfectly capable of tearing any one of us non-dragons to shreds, if given the chance.

I resumed my quiet study of the city beyond the edge of our little hiding place. Some of the daemons were riding pit wolves with charmed iron collars, and others used transportation methods akin to rickshaws maneuvered by weaker, skinnier daemons. There were elites, there were military grunts, there were portly overlords, and there were poor, subjugated daemons. There was a hierarchy, and it sort of put this dark world into perspective.

They had rules and customs, just like the Maras. They lived underground, and they certainly liked it hot. They ate souls and used swamp witch magic. Our problem on Neraka was far more complex than it had seemed at first, and the closer we got to its center, the more layers we discovered as we kept peeling away at it.

"This place is called Black Tower," Caspian whispered, "mainly because of that big one in the middle."

I looked out into the distance and noticed the structure he was talking about. At the very center of the city, a giant tower rose above all the others, thick and round, with a palace serving as a base. The palace was a square construction, each side stretching for half a mile, and was lit up by thousands of little orange flames. It was beautiful and creepy at the same time, and it filled me with dread.

Suddenly, dealing with a handful of invisible hunter daemons seemed like a walk in the park, compared to the fresh hell unraveling in this underground city. My stomach turned into a painful little peanut at the sight of Imen, about a dozen of them, being dragged across one of the lava bridges in cages pulled by pit wolves. They were all females, all young and defenseless. Two daemons snapped their whips at the pit wolves to get them to move faster.

I instinctively moved to help them, but Caspian caught my wrist and pulled me back.

"Don't! We can't risk detection at this point," he murmured.

Glancing to our side, I noticed Hansa, Jax, and even Caia and Blaze nodding, though they weren't happy with that decision either.

"He's right, Harper," Hansa whispered. "There's much more at stake than those Imen girls…"

"So, what, we just let them carry them off so daemons can literally suck the life out of them?" My blood simmered, but deep down, I knew they were right. It just made me feel absolutely miserable.

"This is an evil, violent, and turbulent world, Miss Hellswan," Caspian replied. "The good of the many outweighs the good of the few, and you know it."

I cursed under my breath and gave him a brief, sullen nod in response. Heavy growls sent shivers down my spine, and I looked over the edge again—giant daemons sauntered across another bridge not far from us, pushing the smaller, weaker fiends to the side.

"They're freaking huge," I gasped, my eyes nearly popping out of their orbits as I took in their incredible size. They were twice as big as the daemons we'd encountered before, with double the muscle mass and thick, burly arms and necks. "I bet it would take five or six of us just to tackle one and *maybe* live to see another day…"

"Which is why we need to keep a low profile." Caspian pulled me back again, his grip firm on my right arm. "We need to get to the other side of the city. There's someone there who can help with the information you need to prepare a campaign against the daemons."

"Why won't you spare us the trouble of trekking through a

damn daemon city and give us the information yourself?" I raised an eyebrow at him.

"Because I took an oath of silence on these matters," he finally relented with a deep sigh. He looked at all of us, and shook his head slowly. "You wouldn't understand, but I'll try to explain anyway. As an Exiled Mara and the heir to House Kifo, I take my oaths very seriously, even when everything in my body and conscience tell me otherwise. I swore to keep certain things secret until the right time comes along for me to speak up, but it won't stop me from taking you to see someone who can tell you what I can't. It is the best I can offer, at this point in time."

"How will we get across to the other side of the city, then, given the variety of fiends waiting for us down there?" Blaze frowned.

Caspian pointed at a narrow set of stairs just twenty yards to the right, carved into the wall. They led somewhere below, and were bordered by large, sharp chunks of obsidian.

"We'll go around," he replied. "There are several routes that the daemons barely use in these parts of town. They're narrow enough for us to slip through and kill any fiend we might come across without causing a stir. It'll take us farther to the other side, where we can sneak between huts, undetected."

I braced myself for what came next. My heartrate increased as Caspian took my hand and guided me toward the stairs. The others followed quietly, but I could feel the tension mounting as we descended. The closer we got to the daemons, the harder it was to breathe.

Whatever came next, we had to pull through. Caspian's hold on me helped a little, soothing some of my frayed nerves; it was enough for me to focus and use my True Sight along the way, looking out for daemons who might get too close and see us through the obsidian gaps. Down here, nobody bothered to hide.

Down here, the daemons could be themselves, and we were the ones hiding.

Oh, how the roles have changed...

20

SCARLETT

(DAUGHTER OF JERAMIAH & PIPPA)

W e'd been scouring the city library's archives for several hours. Patrik looked through all the scientific papers available, while I took notes from pages of local lore—though we only had the Exiled Maras' written words to go on. There was absolutely nothing from the Imen's culture.

Patrik nervously flipped through the pages of a science journal that analyzed the effects of the asteroid belt on the Nerakian fauna and flora. There were patterns that the ancient Maras had identified, but they mostly concerned the impact of the asteroids in conjunction with the alignment of the three moons. He was beginning to lose patience, and it wasn't like him.

"Are you okay?" I asked, taking a quick break from my notes. My survey of local lore hadn't yielded any useful insights, other than the Maras' suspicion that the asteroids influenced dreams during certain periods of time.

"Not really," Patrik replied, pinching the bridge of his nose, a clear sign that tension was building up inside him. "I just can't find anything useful. There's no data on how to potentially disrupt the asteroids' effect on communications and spells, but there are plenty of hypotheses on how they actually affect the planet. It's like the Maras have plenty of information on the problem, but absolutely nothing on a solution."

I looked down at my book, a three-hundred-year-old volume of folklore, and sighed. I had nothing to offer him either, but we couldn't stop searching. We had to find a way to reach out to Calliope, and we definitely needed a way off the planet, sooner rather than later.

"I don't think we're done here yet," I offered. "We'll find something eventually. It has to be in here somewhere..."

"What if it isn't?" He frowned, concern darkening his steely blue eyes. "What if this is all there is? What if we find nothing and I have no means of helping our team with those wretched asteroids? What if these are my limits?"

"Patrik, it's not... I don't think it will come to that," I replied, not liking his hopelessness. Patrik was our beacon of light, the Druid with enough knowledge to get us out of any conundrum, no matter how difficult. It wasn't in his nature to be so negative and frustrated, and it clawed at my stomach to see him like this. "I think we need a bit more patience, and to exhaust all our options here before we start looking elsewhere. It's what we do…"

He leaned against the back of his chair and crossed his arms over his chest, sulking. His breathing was heavy, judging by how his chest moved up and down. His brow furrowed, and a vein started pulsating in his temple. He was getting anxious, even angry, and I had no idea what I could do to get him out of that state.

Anger never produced results, or even any good ideas. It was a destructive emotion and adverse to a Druid's ethos.

"What if this is it? What if we're stuck here for the rest of our lives?" Patrik muttered.

I shook my head, instantly rejecting that premise. There was no way that was happening. My family, my friends… my life… It was all back in The Shade and on Calliope, with GASP. I had no intention of spending an eternity on Neraka, surrounded by daemons and secretive Maras and brainwashed Imen. The mere concept of such powerlessness made my stomach churn in painful ways.

"That's not happening, Patrik," I replied, feeling my muscles tense and harden under the pressure of such grim thoughts.

"I'm feeling so damn helpless right now, Scarlett." He looked at me, the pained look on his face too much for me to handle. "I should be able to fix this somehow. I should be able to help my team get through this, and I'm just so… powerless. How do I make this right?"

He was so nervous and insecure—I'd never seen this side of

Patrik. On one hand it was endearing to see him in this light, to know he had weak spots despite his prowess in the magical arts. But it really wasn't going to help us now. I needed Patrik at the top of his game.

I exhaled deeply and decided to do something that would disrupt his current state.

I need to shock him somehow...

"There's nothing here to—" He tried to speak, but I cupped his face and kissed him, pressing my lips against his for a few deliciously long seconds. It was the only thing I could think of. And it felt so good. Time seemed to stop as I relished the sensation produced by his lips. His skin was so soft against my fingertips, I had a hard time letting go.

My heart fluttered in my chest, the taste of him lingering on my lips long after I pulled myself back. I needed a moment to catch my breath, my eyes closed as I struggled to regain my composure. The effect that Patrik had on me was far more powerful than I'd thought, and the kiss was vivid proof, as my brain had switched off.

Not a single thought passed through my head for about a minute, but my blood simmered. Tingling sensations traveled through my chest, gathering in my stomach before they dissolved into a peculiar but wonderful warmth spreading all over.

I opened my eyes and found Patrik staring at me, dumbfounded. His lips were parted, and his heart thundered in his chest, the frantic beating captured by my vampire senses. He was speechless, and I couldn't help but smile softly.

"What... What..." he managed, his voice barely audible. He blinked several times, trying to make sense of what had just happened.

"I had to do something." I shrugged, my cheeks catching fire. "You were spiraling out of control with all that negativity. I'm sorry..."

"No, don't... I..."

His eyes lit up, and he lost his train of thought along the way. I knew that look. He had an idea.

"I know what to do," he mumbled, straightening his back.

I can't believe it worked...

"You do?" I croaked, now realizing the full impact that kissing him had on me. Ironically, he was snapping back to his old self, the confident Patrik that I'd fallen for, while I was melting on the inside, unable to string together a single coherent thought.

"Yes, I... I think I've got it." He stood, reenergized and downright beaming with excitement. He took my hands and pulled me up to my feet, closing the distance between us to the point where barely a few inches separated our lips. "Thank you, Scarlett. It was a strange method you employed to snap me out of it, but it worked. We'll have to talk about this later, but for now... we need to go."

I nodded slowly, losing myself in his gaze for a split second before he guided me out of the reading room and back to the library's main reception. He'd said we'd talk about it later, but what did that mean? Was I in some sort of trouble?

Pretty sure you've been in trouble since you first laid eyes on him, girl...

"There's an ancient Druid spell I can use," he said as we rushed down the circular staircase leading toward the main hall. "It's part of the forbidden dark arts scrolls that Draven found at Stonewall, and it didn't immediately spring to mind, but I think I can perform it here. I can aim it at the asteroid belt directly and try to disrupt its flow in space, but I'll need some ingredients for it... Certain crystals and herbs."

"Do you think the Maras have them?" I asked, finally able to speak as the concept of a forbidden spell set in. It meant we actually stood a chance after all.

"They might, if they brought some with them from Calliope," he replied as we reached the reception desk. "If not, I could try to replace them with local ingredients and try the spell at a shorter range first, just to test it until I get the formula right. Either way, you were right, Scarlett. We can do this."

My heart was doing expert somersaults at that point, as I was thrilled to have been able to give Patrik the support he desperately needed during such trying times. It filled me with a kind of happiness that I'd never experienced before. The Imen currently working in reception shifted their focus to us, producing faint but warm smiles.

"How can we help you?" one of them asked.

"I was wondering where we could find certain crystals,

powders, and plants that the Maras may have brought over from Calliope when they first arrived here," Patrik replied. "Surely they must have brought stuff over that wasn't endemic to Neraka, right?"

The two Imen looked at each other, then back at us, and nodded.

"You might find what you're looking for at the Spring Fair," the first Iman said. "It just so happens that it starts tomorrow."

"Ah, we'll have to wait until tomorrow." Patrik shook his head with disappointment.

"Well, you can also try Master Specter's store on the first level, if you're in a hurry," the second Iman replied. "He usually opens a stall during the Spring Fair, as well. You could check with him first before the Spring Fair. He closes at midnight, so you still have some time."

"Thank you." Patrik beamed at the Imen with renewed enthusiasm, then gave me a confident wink. "Let's go see Master Specter."

He kept holding my hand as we left the library and rushed down the alleys and stone steps leading to the first level. The evening had set in cool shades of purple in the sky, the street-lamps were lit, and people had begun to scatter away to their homes.

My pulse raced as I followed Patrik, his touch making my arm tingle. I couldn't believe I'd actually kissed him. My courage had come out of nowhere, and it had disappeared just as fast. But I'd kissed Patrik, and the feeling that lingered over my lips was proof that I hadn't imagined it.

I held my breath whenever he glanced at me. All I could think of were the consequences of my gesture. How did this change the dynamic between us? Would it have a negative impact? Was he going to tell me I made a mistake?

Did I, though? Did I make a mistake? Or am I just overthinking this?

How couldn't I overthink it? I'd just freakin' kissed Patrik.

21

AVRIL

(DAUGHTER OF LUCAS & MARION)

W e looked around on the third level of the city, asking the occasional passing Iman to show us where Lemuel's bookstore was. One young Iman girl pointed us the right way, and, shortly after we'd left Cynara and Hera back at the South Bend Inn, we found the old Iman's place.

The lights were off. Heron and I quickly circled the house, listening and looking for any sign of movement inside, but the place was empty.

"We need to get inside, though," I said, checking to see if anyone was coming by. Lemuel's house was on a relatively secluded street, and the evening shade did a pretty good job of further concealing it. "I have to catch his scent from an object he has touched."

"Okay, I can help with that." Fiona smirked and produced a

pin from her hair, which she used to pick the lock on the main door, while Heron and I kept a lookout.

The lock's mechanism surrendered with a click, and Fiona pushed the door open. We went inside and began our survey of the place, without turning any lights on. The bookstore was on the ground floor—a quaint little place with wooden shelves and racks loaded with a variety of books, scrolls, and literary papers. Judging by the titles, there were some Imen works being sold; the Imen author names carried the mention of their species on the covers. I figured the titles were necessary to differentiate between the Maras and Imen.

There was a small reception desk in a corner, behind a circular staircase leading upstairs. Farther to the right, there was a kitchen area separated from the bookstore with a wooden panel, on which various literary scenes were illustrated in broad and colorful brush strokes. The opposite corner held a reading space, complete with a bench and two velvet armchairs, and molten candles on a side table.

Heron followed me upstairs, while Fiona kept looking through the shelves.

"Maybe there's something useful here about the asteroid belt," she whispered before I started up the stairs.

"Fair enough," I replied. "I'll look for something of Lemuel's in the meantime."

The top floor was spacious and modestly furnished, with a bedroom, an open living room, a kitchenette, and a tiled bathroom. I found a coat thrown on the armrest of one of the lounge chairs, and briefly sniffed it. Lemuel's scent reminded me of crisp autumn mornings, a mixture of burnt wood, fallen leaves, and crushed grapes filling my senses.

"Got it?" Heron watched me, his jade eyes flickering with curiosity. I gave him a brief nod, and he moved back toward the stairs. "Let's go, then."

I followed him back to the ground floor, where Fiona was sifting through the bookshelves, checking each volume carefully before putting it back.

"We're going to track Lemuel," I said slowly. "Do you want to stay here and keep looking through the books, Fi? Or do you want to come with us? It's up to you."

"I'll stay here." She gave me a reassuring smile. "If anything, I'll see you two later, at the infirmary. I've got that dinner to get to, anyway, so I'll just hang out here until it's time to go change."

"Ah, yes, you'll have to get all pretty and fabulous to knock Vincent off his feet." Heron grinned playfully, and I gave up on nudging him for his taunts. I actually found his banter attempts cute, even endearing at times. His sense of humor and light-heartedness made our compulsory stay on Neraka a bit more bearable.

"At least I'll be treated to a fancy dinner and not be roaming through this wretched city at night, unlike *other* people I know," Fiona shot back, wiggling her eyebrows.

I chuckled as we left her in the bookstore and took to the streets to look for Lemuel. His scent lingered heavily in the air, and I could confidently follow it down the alley leading into the western part of the third level.

"Do you think Lemuel is keeping those hidden archives back there?" Heron asked as we walked through a thinning crowd of Imen and Maras. Most were going home, but some wore black uniforms and were headed to the city's inns and bars for the night shift—I could tell from the crisp scent of fresh laundry, along with the fragrances and other toiletries they'd used to look their part as servants in certain establishments.

"In the bookstore, you mean?" I asked, and he replied with a nod. "Maybe, but not in plain sight, and we don't have Harper to help us with her True Sight. If he's keeping them at his place, they're well hidden. Lemuel doesn't strike me as a careless Iman, based on what scents I caught in his house."

"What do you mean?"

"Well, he uses a lot of detergents around the place, and those substances can really throw a tracker's nose off the grand prize," I said. "It's why I needed to sniff his coat to get a good trail. You wouldn't notice it at first, but that bookstore would normally smell like old books, ink soaked into pages, and even a little mold and dust from the older stuff he keeps in there. But it smells of... brandy and lime, incense and something akin to bleach. That place was scrubbed clean."

"Maybe he was doing some spring cleaning in there." Heron gave me an amused sideways glance as we turned left into another alley.

We passed a local tavern and a couple of stores, and Lemuel's scent got stronger.

"Not with that many cleaning products." I smirked. "It's a masking tactic that some animals use to throw predators off their tracks. It's used by species across the worlds we know, and this one is no exception. The scents I caught in his house were strong and permanent, seeping into the structural beams and every other inch of wood in there. He's definitely hiding something."

"That nose of yours is fantastic, I swear." Heron shook his head slowly, amazed. "I mean, I thought I was a good tracker, but then you came along. I am literally in awe of you."

"Thank you." I gave him a warm smile, feeling my cheeks burn under his intense gaze. "I was always fascinated with chemistry and the olfactory sense... The two just came naturally to me, I guess. When I was given the option to further hone this skill, I took it."

"It's a good thing you did." He nodded. "Your contributions so far have been extraordinary."

"Well, I wouldn't say *that,* but yeah, I guess I can hold my own on this team." I giggled, trying to maintain some sense of modesty under his barrage of compliments.

A couple of minutes went by in absolute silence. I stole a glance at Heron, and he looked as though he were trying to say something, but couldn't find the right words.

"Avril," he finally spoke, "have you ever thought about a soulmate?"

The question made me feel nervous, mainly because I didn't understand its purpose, but also because I found myself instinctively looking at him as I tried to formulate an answer. My feelings for him were developing at an alarmingly rapid pace, and I knew, deep down, that my answer would be yes.

"What do you mean?" I asked.

"I mean, have you thought about having someone in your life, someone you'd want to spend an eternity with?" His gaze was clouded as he studied my expression, and I felt vulnerable all of a sudden.

"No... Yes... Okay, yes, I have thought about it." I surrendered. What was the point in lying, anyway? We were stuck on this planet, and the future was so murky, so unclear, it felt like a disservice to myself if I denied it. *You only get one life, and so on...*

"What would that person be like?" he replied, then stared at the road ahead. The streetlamps cast a yellowish light over the cobblestone, and long shadows crossed the alley from various angles.

"I haven't given it *that* much thought, but... I don't know, if I were to make up a profile right now, off the top of my head, I guess he'd have to be someone who can accept me exactly the way I am... my curiosity, my strong opinions, and my quirks included."

Heron didn't say anything for a while, and, upon analyzing what I'd just said, I realized my statement felt incomplete.

"Of course," I continued, "I would reciprocate. I'd accept him. I'd... love him, both his good and bad sides. I just can't get more specific because, to be honest, I'm still trying to figure it out. I've never been in love with anyone before, Heron. I don't know what that's supposed to feel like, exactly. I also know I've got a very long life ahead of me, and I just don't see myself rushing into anything..."

That was my defense mechanism rearing its not-so-pretty head. Alarm signals went off whenever I looked at Heron, opposing the butterflies squirming in my stomach and the frantic beats of my heart. He nodded slowly. I caught a glimpse of what seemed like disappointment in his eyes as he looked down and scratched the back of his neck.

"That... That makes sense," he muttered.

I stilled and caught his forearm, stopping him in his tracks. Something felt a little off.

"What's up?" he whispered.

"I think we're being followed," I replied, then looked over my shoulder.

The street was getting crowded with dozens of Imen of all ages. There must have been a gathering of sorts nearby. I started walking but didn't let go of Heron's arm. We slipped through the stream of people and made a sharp left turn, hiding between the walls of two neighboring houses.

The space was narrow, forcing Heron to stand extremely close to me. His chest pressed against mine, and I felt the heat from his hard body simmering into me. Our proximity seemed to affect us both, as he lowered his head slowly. I was looking to the right when I felt his breath on my cheek and turned my head, my nose touching his.

I found myself drowning in his jade eyes. His hands rested on my hips. The world gradually dissolved around us, and I found comfort in the shield of his body for a few moments. We stayed like that for what seemed like eons, until his lips inched closer and almost touched mine. My heart jumped in my throat as I struggled to breathe. I wanted him to kiss me—so badly that I nearly missed Lemuel's scent getting stronger.

"He's here," I croaked, my lips parting beneath his.

Heron was losing control, but he tried to make sense of what I'd just said, while his eyes were fixed on mine.

"Wha... What?" he managed.

"Lemuel is here. He's coming this way," I whispered.

He lifted his head and looked out into the street. His arm shot out just as an old Iman passed by us. Heron grabbed him by his lapel and pulled him into the tight space with us. Lemuel whimpered as Heron immobilized him, pushing him against the wall.

Our little hiding spot was suddenly even more crowded, and I was too close to Heron for my mind to stay clear—and that was a challenge, because we'd just found Lemuel, as he'd followed us around. I shook my head and forced myself back into focus.

"We're not going to hurt you," I said softly.

Lemuel squirmed and tried to free himself, but he didn't stand a chance against Heron. The old Iman froze when he realized he was dealing with a Mara. The horror on his face was almost heartbreaking—this creature was terrified of Heron's kind, and I knew it had something to do with the Exiled Maras.

"Don't... Please... I wasn't looking to do any harm..." Lemuel breathed, his eyes wide and glassy. He was in his late sixties, tufts of white hair poking out from beneath his dark brown hat, wrinkles drawing shadows across his features. His body trembled with fear, and I put my hand on his shoulder to try to calm him down.

"We're not going to hurt you, I promise." I felt the need to repeat myself. "Why were you following us?"

"I saw you coming out of my house," Lemuel replied, his voice barely audible. The crowd in the street was quite loud—a mixture of laughter and friendly words as the Imen praised the quality of a play they'd just watched, based on the fragments of theater-related conversation that trickled into our nook. "I just wanted to know what you were looking for..."

"We were looking for you, Lemuel," I said, keeping my tone as gentle as possible. "Cynara and Hera told us where to find you. We need your help."

"I... How could I possibly help *you*?"

"We need to see the Imen archives you've been keeping away from the Maras," Heron replied. "The girls told us you're quite the collector."

"How... How did you know? Did they tell you? How did you know to ask them about..." Lemuel's voice trailed off, and his jaw dropped. "Hera and Cynara willingly told you? How is that possible?"

"Because they wanted to help us help them... help you, and every other innocent creature in this city," I said. "We need to read those archives; we need to understand what the Imen know about the daemons, in particular. The Maras don't know anything, and they're getting killed off one by one by these monsters. We're going to end this, once and for all, but we need all the information you can give us about them."

"But... But it's just old wives' tales... folklore, legends, and myths... I don't know how it could help." The old Iman shook his head slowly.

"It doesn't matter. We need to read everything you have," I replied. "Please, you have to help us. We have a shot at bringing this to an end, but we need your help."

Lemuel looked away, avoiding Heron's persistent gaze. I had a feeling he was afraid of getting mind-bent.

"I... I can't... If I reveal the archives, my people will be in trouble." He sighed, his bony shoulders dropping.

"How? Why?" I asked, and Lemuel looked at us with confusion, his brow furrowed.

"I... I don't know. I just know I have to keep it a secret. No one can know."

"I can mind-bend it out of you right now if I want to," Heron warned him. "But I won't. I am asking you nicely. *We* are asking you nicely because we trust you. Trust *us*, too. We have no intention of telling anyone anything about your archives. We don't work for the Maras, and we don't work for you. All we want to do is stop the daemons from attacking your city."

The old Iman gave it some thought, his worried gaze darting between Heron and me. He eventually gave us both a brief nod, and Heron moved back, releasing him.

"We simply need to know more about the written history of your people," I added, "daemons and all. Please, help us."

"I don't keep them at the bookstore," Lemuel conceded. "Come with me."

He left the narrow space between houses, and we followed him back down the alley from which we'd come. Heron moved to his left side, and I kept to his right, keeping him between us, both to protect him and to quickly restrain him if he decided to run off.

"Where do you keep them, then?" I asked.

"I have a studio on the first level," Lemuel replied. I frowned slightly, wondering why he'd gone to such efforts to conceal any clandestine scents in his bookstore, if the archive wasn't even there. "I couldn't risk a raid, so I purchased a floor in a small townhouse below, under my niece's name. I keep everything there."

"Then what are you hiding in the bookstore?" I muttered, making sure no passersby overheard us. Lemuel gave me a surprised look, and I raised my eyebrow at him. "Come on, you've doused the place in cleaning solutions repeatedly, and, judging by the mess in your house upstairs, you're not exactly a germaphobe."

"A germ-what?" He blinked several times in confusion.

"Answer the question, Lemuel," Heron interjected, his voice firm as he scowled at the old Iman.

"I... I can't tell you."

"I can *make* you tell me," Heron shot back.

"Okay, just don't make me tell you *here*. Have some patience, and I will explain!" Lemuel was getting frustrated and grouchy. I stifled a grin and gave Heron a sideways glance. He, too, was slightly amused.

Lemuel was the typical grumpy old dude who didn't like being questioned and whose survival instincts had probably kept him alive up until now. From what I remembered, based on the interviews we'd had with House Roho's servants, few Imen lived past the age of forty or fifty. I had a feeling Lemuel knew a lot more than what he was telling us, but he was right. We were in the middle of an alley filled with people. It wasn't the right time to discuss such details.

As night fell, the sky got darker and stars twinkled over-head, trailing the first moon. We escorted Lemuel down to the first level, deep in the bowels of the so-called slums of the city.

The streets got narrower, with fewer light sources. Heron and I ended up walking next to each other, Lemuel in front of us.

"It's just two hundred feet away," the old Iman said.

My arms brushed against Heron's occasionally, sparking tingling sensations that rushed through my whole body, then gathered in the back of my throat.

We'd almost kissed, and I didn't know what to do with that anymore. Was it just a moment's impulse? Or was Heron orbiting toward me for some reason? Either way, the more I thought about it, the more anxious I got. The more I wanted a kiss to actually happen.

I'd felt his lips against mine back at Jovi and Anjani's wedding.

And that's something impossible to forget...

22

FIONA

(DAUGHTER OF BENEDICT & YELENA)

I lost track of time while sifting through Lemuel's bookshelves, and came up empty. There wasn't a single book in there discussing the asteroid belt from a more scientific perspective—just lots of useless lore. It seemed as though the Maras had actually brought some impressive development to the planet. The Imen seemed quite primitive and gullible, holding their legends and ritualistic beliefs in high regard, while the Maras opted for scientific and technological advancement. Swamp witch magic seemed like one of the few things both species agreed on as very much real.

I moved to another shelf, and looked at the titles. Mostly folklore about water spirits and deities that influenced the weather. The Imen had gathered an impressive culture throughout their millennia on this planet.

Hot air brushed against the back of my neck, and I instantly jolted to the side, pulling my sword out on instinct. I wasn't alone in here. My heart thudded violently against my ribs as I briefly scanned my surroundings and noticed the air rippling in the reading corner.

"Don't come any closer!" I called out, my voice firm and filled with the promise of death, while I looked for a water source to use against the daemon.

"Would it make you more comfortable if I revealed myself?"

That voice... It sounded awfully familiar. My spine tingled, and the air seemed to thicken around me as I watched a vase get lifted off a corner table. The daemon took the flowers out, tossing them onto the floor, and poured the water over his tall and broad frame, revealing himself.

I held my breath. I recognized Zane, standing in the freaking bookstore, just a few feet away from me. He was as tall as I remembered him, his muscles heavy and toned, and his chest and arms covered in tribal tattoos. What was he doing in the city?

What is he doing here? Oh no, is he here to take me away again? Not happening!

I kept my sword out, my grip tightening around the handle to the point where my hand trembled a little. There was no way in hell I was letting him drag me back to those wretched gorges again.

Zane cocked his head to one side, a flicker of amusement lighting up his fiery red eyes.

"Relax, Fiona, I'm not here to take you away," he said, his voice gruff and sending some very mixed signals to my brain. "Although I could, since the dragon's out of town."

"No longer surprised that you know so much about our movements," I muttered, taking a couple of steps back to increase the distance between us. My throat closed up in his presence, the intensity weighing heavily on my shoulders. There was something about him that demanded my full attention and... not fear, but rather... respect. "What are you doing here, Zane? What do you want?"

A couple of seconds went by. He took his time to formulate an answer as he measured me from head to toe with renewed interest.

"I'm just... visiting." He shrugged, his gaze settled on my face, while I had trouble keeping my eyes on his. The sinuous curves of his shoulders, the deep lines of his hips as they sank beneath the massive leather belt, the ropes of muscle threaded down his abdomen—they all required attention. "It's been a while since we've seen each other, and, by the looks of you, I bet you missed me."

His smirk set me off. My cheeks burned, and I snapped out of my split second daze, shifting my focus back to his red eyes. He'd caught me staring, and I hated it.

"It's been a while since we saw each other?" I mockingly repeated his statement with a raised eyebrow. "You saw me just yesterday."

"And today couldn't come soon enough." He grinned,

leaning on one of the wooden support beams. He crossed his arms over his chest, and that somehow made him look even bigger. "You look beautiful, by the way. Your stay in the gorge did wonders for your skin."

"What in the world is wrong with you?" I groaned, rolling my eyes. I could not, for the life of me, figure out what his end game was.

"What? I'm just giving you a compliment. Is that a crime?" He raised a patronizing eyebrow at me, further fueling the fire burning in my core. I really wasn't used to such high body temperatures.

"You abducted me. Your species is killing innocent Maras and Imen. You're using magic that you shouldn't even know about, and you are literally stalking me. I'm pretty sure a compliment is kind of useless at this point!"

"I'd dare to disagree." Zane seemed unfazed. "I think it's good to tell the truth, even if it makes people uncomfortable. And the truth is that you look beautiful, and the black leather does you justice."

I blinked several times, trying to wrap my head around what was going on. Why was I just standing here? Why wasn't I looking for the optimum attack angle? And *why* was I blushing?

"I think you've lost your mind somewhere in those gorges." I shook my head slowly.

"Okay, fine, don't take the compliment." Zane scoffed, feigning exasperation. "But either come at me or put that fire poker away before you hurt yourself with it."

"Did you just make fun of my sword?" I narrowed my eyes at him.

Why am I letting him get to me? Snap out of it, Fiona!

He chuckled, then resumed a standing position, putting his hands behind his back.

"You call that a sword?" He pursed his lips.

"Okay, that's it!" I hissed and lunged at him, the blade pointing at his chest.

He expertly dodged it but didn't retaliate. Instead, he stilled and waited for me to come at him again. I wasn't going for the kill, anyway. Something told me that would be nearly impossible. But I needed to assess his fighting skills and, most importantly, his speed.

"That was a bit... weak." He gave me a playful smile.

Oh, really?

I slashed at him again, this time bringing my sword down from the left, and he effortlessly moved back. The blade missed him by inches. He growled with excitement as I launched a flurry of hits, gripping the sword with both hands and swinging it with ample movements that were quite demanding on my shoulder muscles.

Nevertheless, I still couldn't hit him, as he flashed left and right with impressive speed.

We went on like that for a couple of minutes, until I started getting closer. I noticed that the fewer feet between us, the more sluggish his defenses got. Something sparked in the back of my head, and I feigned a hit on the right side, stopped halfway, and immediately executed a rapid 360-degree turn and brought my sword in from the left. I hit nothing but air.

Zane had already vanished in that fraction of a second that I'd turned away.

What the...

"Don't take your eyes off me." His whisper in my right ear made me yelp and jump. His hand came down hard and fast, and knocked the sword out of my hands.

Oh, no, no, no!

Before I knew it, Zane had me with my back against the wall, his massive body pressed against mine as my blade clanged loudly on the wooden floor. That was the sound of defeat I was hearing...

My breath hitched. I couldn't move. His thigh had slipped between my legs, and my arms were twisted and caught behind my back, stuck between my body weight and the wall. *When did he manage to do that?*

I was helpless, my heart pounding out of my chest. Zane looked down at me. His red gaze darkened, his natural fragrance filling my lungs with hints of cedarwood and leather —so intense, almost mesmerizing. I could rip him a new one with my fangs, enough to get my arms out and claw at him like there was no tomorrow. But my instincts were on lockdown. I couldn't react. My brain was working perfectly, but there was something about him that kept me pinned down and motionless.

His breath warmed my face, and his lips stretched into a

lazy smile. What was he going to do now? Most importantly, how was I going to react? Because there was something terribly off about me where Zane was concerned. I had no desire to go for the kill. None whatsoever. He was still, by all possible definitions, the enemy. So why was I so reluctant to treat him as one?

"Do you mind letting go?" I whispered, unable to find my voice.

"I honestly don't know what it is about you," Zane replied, as he sank his face in my hair. I could hear him breathing in deeply, and it made my skin ripple in an eerily pleasant way. My own reaction was baffling. "I can't get enough of your scent. I don't know if it's your soul that smells so good or just you—I'm not sure... but I just had to come see you."

His words sank in slowly, hitting the bottom of my conscience with a loud thud, as I found myself softening against him. My muscles were relaxing, and I couldn't do anything about it. My body was eager to betray me.

"Where did you get the swamp witch magic?" I croaked, changing the subject and trying my best to be a professional. Zane wasn't making it easy at all...

He lifted his head to look at me, his gaze clouded and glimmering crimson. What a fascinating color to look at from up close! His eyes were like round rubies with liquid dashes of gold sprinkled in the middle, and I was slightly hypnotized.

"You just had to ruin the moment, didn't you?" He sighed, shaking his head slowly.

"Well, I need to know," I replied. "You *are* the enemy, after all."

"Am I, though? Besides, you're in over your head. You wouldn't understand, Fiona."

"Ugh, again with that same crappy line," I groaned, manifesting an exaggerated amount of boredom. "Can you please come up with something new?"

He stiffened against me, and I could feel tension building up in his body. He held my arms, his fingers digging into my flesh through the layer of black leather. His gaze darkened as he inched forward, the tip of his nose touching mine.

"You might want to do yourself a favor and stay on my good side, Fiona," he said slowly, his voice rumbling through my stomach. "That is, if you want to survive once it's all over."

"Wait, once *what* is over, exactly?"

He grinned and puffed yellow dust in my face. My brain lit up, but it was too late for me to do anything. *Gah, he expertly conned me!*

I wheezed and choked as everything went dark around me. My body surrendered, and I passed out, once again at Zane's mercy. *Damn...*

23

HARPER

(DAUGHTER OF HAZEL & TEJUS)

We had a limited supply of invisibility paste with us, and we hadn't found any on the daemon we'd captured to get us down here, so we decided to only use it if we had no other choice. We snuck through the outskirts of the city, making good use of all the nooks and crannies in the black stone wall that extended into the massive dome ceiling.

We used stairs and hid behind boulders, taking short one-minute breaks where appropriate, to calculate the next portion of our route and get closer to where Caspian said his friend lived. I had a hard time imagining Caspian's daemon friend, but he certainly wasn't going to be the strangest or craziest thing we'd seen all week.

The lights were always on in this underground city, so there was barely any notion of night and day passing, other than a town clock announcing yet another hour gone. We followed Caspian behind a cluster of dirty old huts, crouching to stay out of sight. Small, weak, and old daemons lived on this side, and they were out and about, growling and grumbling at each other. The occasional insult was hurled, causing the others to snicker at the daemon on the receiving end.

"Call them neighborly pleasantries, if you wish," Caspian muttered, his jade eyes twinkling with amusement when he noticed the frown on my face.

"Yeah, I don't see myself mowing my lawn and saying hello to one of these fellows anytime soon," I replied.

He gave me a half-smile, then reached out to the side of the hut, where a cart was stationed. Several dirty black cloaks were piled up in it—he grabbed them, then handed them over to me, keeping one for himself. I took one, and passed the others to Jax and Hansa, who made sure Caia and Blaze each got a cloak as well.

"Put these on," Caspian whispered. "And keep your heads down. We can pass as weaklings while we move forward. My friend's place is about a hundred yards away from here."

I nodded and covered myself up, then proceeded to follow Caspian as he snuck between rocky huts. A spine-chilling wave of squeals stopped me in my tracks, and I looked over my shoulder to identify the source. Jax, Hansa, Blaze, and Caia stilled next to me as we witnessed the feeding of the poor.

A larger daemon dragged a cart up the narrow road. It was loaded with a cage filled with wild animals the daemon had captured from outside—mostly deer and boar-like creatures that squirmed and whimpered as they got closer to a small gathering of elder daemons.

"Those living in these parts of the city are too weak to hunt for themselves, but they still provide labor," Caspian said, following my gaze. I watched as the cage was flung open, but the animals were too scared to come out. Instead, the daemons went in and started dragging them out, their red eyes glimmering with delight as they tore flesh from bone and ate the meat raw, blood smearing their chins and saggy, wrinkled chests. "So they're fed by the city and kept alive, as they clean up and do various other duties that are considered too demeaning for the others."

"Demeaning?" I murmured, as we continued walking through the poorest parts of the daemon city.

"Yes. Things that hunters and soldiers cannot be tasked with doing. Jobs that are not fit for merchants, servants, and nobles," Caspian replied.

"They have nobles here?" Jax asked, constantly looking around, making sure we weren't followed or noticed.

"Of course," Caspian said. "They have hierarchies in place, like an organized society, and that includes royal and noble blood."

We followed him deeper into a section of rounded, igloo-shaped huts made from black obsidian blocks. They looked cleaner and smoother than what we'd seen so far. The daemons here were quiet and kept away from the crowded main street that stretched about fifty yards to our left.

"This is where clerics live," Caspian explained. "The others leave them alone, mainly because the king likes them. Their service to local deities isn't valued in any way, but the king is amused and fascinated by their ancient customs, which long precede him, so he leaves them be."

"You're awfully chatty about daemons now," I noticed, raising an eyebrow at him.

He gave me a brief sideways glance as I kept up with him.

"These aren't secrets anymore. You are here, walking among them. The least I can do is explain what you're seeing," he replied bluntly. "Anyway, we are here."

We stopped in front of a small hut. Caspian checked our surroundings, and then we went inside. The place looked nice and rather spacious. Orange lights flickered on wall-mounted shells, and furs lined the floor. There were several crates piled on one side, and a small firepit dug in the middle. It was currently being used for boiling water infused with pleasant-smelling herbs.

An old daemon shot to his feet as soon as he saw us, a glimmer of recognition in his eyes at the sight of Caspian, followed by concern as he measured each of us from head to toe.

"It's okay, Mose," Caspian said. "They're here to help the Nerakians."

Mose looked to be in his mid-sixties, his long black hair

riddled with thick white streaks pouring into a ponytail. Red and yellow beads were braided into the hair on top of his head, and he wore a simple black tunic that left only his arms and calves uncovered. There was a medallion around his neck that caught my eye—a silver triangle mounted in a circle, with a black enamel center on which a familiar symbol had been painted red.

"Are they the ones you spoke of, Lord Kifo?" Mose asked, taking several wary steps forward to get a better look at us.

"Yes, Mose. We need to talk," Caspian replied, as Mose motioned for us to sit around the firepit and pulled a black curtain over the hut's entrance, before he sat down across the fire from us.

"What are you all doing here?" Mose asked, his red eyes on Caspian.

"I'm under oath and cannot tell them everything they need to know, but you can help fill in some of the blanks," Caspian said, his knee touching mine as he crossed his legs in his seated position.

Silence fell between us for a minute, while I tried to read Mose's emotions. I'd not had any luck with the other daemons I'd encountered, and Mose was just as immune to my sentry abilities. My shoulders dropped. I'd known the chances were slim, but still, can't blame a girl for trying...

"What do you wish to know?" Mose eventually asked, his gaze fixed on me. "You can ask, instead of trying to poke around in my head."

My cheeks flushed as I realized he'd felt me just then.

"So you can sense when I try to read your mind," I mumbled, and Mose responded with a nod.

"You can't read me, but I can definitely feel you trying," he replied. "Word's already out about you, young lady. The hunters you faced came back with interesting stories."

"Okay then, let's start with some basics." I leaned forward. "How old are you, Mose?"

"Seventy-one thousand, nine-hundred, and ninety-nine full moons. And I've yet to know your name, young lady."

I blinked several times, doing quick math in my head.

"My apologies. I am Harper," I said, then nodded at the rest of our team. "These are Jax, Hansa, Caia, and Blaze. We are members of GASP. And you're... six thousand years old?"

"I believe so, yes," Mose replied, looking at each of us for a couple of seconds, as if putting our names to our faces. His gaze settled on Jax. "You're a Mara."

"Yes, I am," Jax said.

"But you're not from here."

"No, I'm from Calliope."

"Ah, the world from which our Nerakian Maras were exiled." Mose scoffed, the shadow of a smile flickering over his face.

"Tell us about your species," I said, content with having the lead in this conversation. There were *so* many questions I wanted to ask.

"That's a broad request," Mose smirked, "but I will do my

best to tell you as much as I can, without putting my own life at risk."

"What, so you're under oath, too, or something?" I frowned, already sensing I wouldn't get all the answers I'd hoped for.

"We all answer to higher powers in this world, Miss Harper. But, to answer your request, we are daemons. Our kind has inhabited this world since the beginning of time. We inhabited cities beneath the surface of Neraka—hundreds of them, linked by tunnels spanning hundreds, even thousands of miles."

Jax rubbed the back of his neck, cringing as he heard the painfully unpleasant truth: there were more daemons out there than we'd thought. We definitely couldn't take them all on by ourselves.

"You mean to tell me there are more of you out there?" Jax replied.

"Yes. Tens of thousands." Mose nodded. "But this is the capital city. It is the home of our king, Shaytan, ruler of all daemons. We thrive in the underground, away from the sunlight, bathed in volcanic heat."

"Yeah, I can see that," Hansa shot back, wiping the sweat from her face. I wasn't too far behind her as far as level of discomfort, and, judging by the glistening beads forming on Caspian's temple, he was coming in third, along with Jax. Blaze and Caia seemed comfortable.

Figures...

"What about soul eating?" I asked.

"We feed on souls. I'm not sure what is unclear about that."

Mose shrugged. "In the absence of souls, however, we eat raw flesh. When we are young, we are able to hunt and provide for ourselves, especially where souls are concerned. The older we get, however, the weaker our bodies become, and we're reduced to eating meat. In this day and age, becoming old and not being royalty, military, or nobility, you are automatically bumped to the bottom of the food chain and reduced to living in these slums, taking the mercy food that hunters bring in from the surface."

"Like the cages we saw outside, stuffed with living, wild animals," I muttered with disgust.

"Yes. And I'd say that beats eating souls, don't you think?" Mose retorted. I gave him a brief nod. "What you probably do not understand about soul eating is how exhilarating it can be. One soul can keep you sated for days, even weeks on end. Raw meat barely gets us through the day. We don't experience hunger like the Imen do. Our stomachs do not ache for sustenance. Our entire bodies do. Soul eating is painfully addictive, Miss Harper, and weaning off it can be deadly. We need plenty of raw meat to quench some of the urges. So, yes, our city helps us—as long as we prove to be useful. Once we are no longer able to support our society in any way, we are no longer fed."

"Survival of the fittest taken to a new extreme, I see," I replied. "Survival of the useful, sounds more like it. And after all these years of service, are daemons just okay with being tossed aside like that?"

"They don't have a choice. That is how our world works."

Mose shrugged, with a tinge of sadness in his voice. "The day will come when I will experience that same end. Just not yet. I still have a few years ahead of me, and I plan to put them to good use."

"Is that why you're helping us?" Jax asked.

"Not exactly. To tell you the truth, soul eating wasn't always a part of our nature as daemons. It started out about... ten, eleven thousand years ago. We don't know who discovered it and how; it just became the norm. It has turned my people into beasts, a degenerate mass of violent soul eaters, and we've systematically reduced the Imen's population on the surface of Neraka. There used to be millions of them..."

There was a collective gasp among us as we came to terms with the horrible truth. The Imen were the primary targets of daemons, and they were nearing extinction because of this soul eating practice.

"Since the Imen population has been dwindling, my people have resorted to feeding off the Maras lately," Mose continued, shaking his head with contempt. "I swore off souls a long time ago... not because I couldn't hunt anymore, but because I saw the cruelty of our ways. I couldn't do it anymore. Of course, I'm a mere underling, a nobody. No one noticed when I got clean. The same cannot be said about the others, higher up."

"Higher up?" I asked.

"I'm part of the slums. The workers and the dying old. Well, technically I'm a cleric, as I preserve the daemon lore archives for the king's reading pleasure, but I still go out and clean the streets if needed. I do not wish to live at the mercy of an insane monarch. Above us are the soldiers, the armored daemons. The military is a key part of our society. They enforce laws and some sense of order. Then come the hunters, given invisibility magic so they can go out to the surface and fetch us our food. There are thousands of them. They start off by hunting animals for us, and they get paid in souls. Once they become strong enough, they can choose to become independent hunters, and provide sustenance for themselves and their children only."

"Daemons raise families?" Jax replied, frowning as he probably tried to imagine a daemon family scene. I was doing the same and, for the life of me, no clear picture came to mind.

"Not exactly," Mose said. "The males choose their females to mate. The females are given custody of the child for the first seven years, then the males take them away to raise them strong and teach them how to survive in our society."

"And what happens to the females after that?" Hansa asked, her gaze slowly darkening as her hands balled into fists.

"They're chosen by other males to produce more children. Once the children reach adulthood, they are given options for what to do with their lives. Most of the females go on to bear children of their own, but some become hunters or even join the military."

A few minutes went by as the picture began to clear, as far as the daemon society was concerned. Their behavior started making sense, but it didn't make me want to sympathize with any of them. If anything, it made my stomach churn harder at the thought of mothers being forced to separate from their children like that. It was downright heartbreaking...

"We saw some huge daemons out there," Jax then said. "Much bigger than the... hunters, and even the armored fiends we've seen on the surface. What are they? They must have some special role."

"Yes, they're Legions." Mose nodded, fear flickering in his eyes. "Generals that command our armies. There are dozens of them in each city, and believe me, you do not wish to cross them. Sometimes, they get involved in hard labor just to show the others that they can get down and dirty despite their high rank. It's our military's way of keeping its soldiers rooted. Nobody wants an arrogant mass of muscle thinking he's better than others in his rank. And the Legions answer to the Seven Princes, the seven sons of Shaytan. His firstborn sons, to be precise, because the king spawns dozens of offspring each year, but only the first seven are granted a chance at the throne. He's been around for three thousand years now, though, and he's not going away anytime soon."

"So the Seven Princes command the military?" I asked.

"Not just the military," Mose replied. "They form the Council in charge of the day-to-day running of our kingdom and our capital city. Their younger brothers are assigned to the other cities, in equal groups of seven."

"How many sons does Shaytan have?" Caia's eyes widened.

"Honestly, we've lost track. He takes some new wife every two years or so. He has dozens of those already, so he is never short of heirs. He doesn't discard the wives after they give birth; he likes his palace rooms filled with beautiful females and his offspring, I suppose." Mose shrugged. "But it's the Seven Princes who call the shots and help him govern. I will give you their names, so you know who to target when your armies come to Neraka."

"Yeah, I'm not sure that's—"

"That is very kind of you. Thank you, Mose," Caspian interrupted me. I bit my tongue then, realizing that we couldn't risk our one ally on the daemon side learning of our hopefully temporary issue with getting GASP over to Neraka.

"The first born is Cayn. He is ruthless and has a filthy soul. He will most likely succeed his father on the throne. The second is Abeles, followed by Garros, Mammon, Karellen, Adaris, and the youngest on the Council, Zane. They are very different but share common goals, which is why the Council ultimately works in passing decisions around the kingdom. King Shaytan signs off on all of them, though."

"Are there other species inhabiting Neraka?" Caia then asked. "Aside from the Imen, Maras, and daemons, that is. Perhaps fae, swamp witches?" Jax, Hansa, Blaze, Caspian, and I looked at her with confusion, and she gave us a defensive shrug. "What? I'm just trying all avenues here, because this whole swamp witch magic thing still doesn't make sense to me, and neither does Vesta's presence!"

Caia was still trying to wrap her head around the fae who had helped us in the Valley of Screams during our rescue mission. To be honest, we were just as baffled as she was, and the fact that Vesta didn't know anything about her past only served to amplify the mystery around her.

"It used to be a much livelier planet, I'll tell you *that*." Mose sighed. "There were other creatures living on the surface, but I don't know what became of them. I haven't seen their kind in centuries. I suppose that's what happens when daemons become the dominant species... We consume everything in our path..."

"What can you tell us about them?" Caia replied.

Mose's head turned as he picked up noises from outside. His eyes flared bright red, and he looked at us, fear draining the color from his face.

"Quick, hide! The crates," he whispered, and we scrambled to our feet. Voices became clearer outside the hut.

"What's happening, Mose?" Caspian breathed, visibly confused.

"They've come for me," the old daemon replied, motioning for us to hurry. Caia, Blaze, Jax, and Hansa were the first to hide behind the stack of crates, several feet away from the firepit.

"What do you mean? Why?" Caspian frowned, then pushed me to join the rest of my team. I stumbled and landed on top of Hansa, who groaned and helped me back to my feet. We all crouched.

"Nothing for you to worry about." Mose shook his head as he nudged Caspian into our hiding spot. "Just stay hidden, and, if I don't make it back, you keep going with our plan, Lord Kifo. Just keep going."

"Wait, how can I *not* worry if you follow up with 'if I don't come back', Mose?" Caspian was frustrated, and I felt the need to hold his arm, just to make sure he wouldn't leave my side.

Mose grabbed a metal bowl and scooped ashes from the dying firepit, which he scattered over us. I covered my mouth and nose so as not to choke on it, while we all huddled closer together.

"This will keep your scent hidden in closed quarters with daemons," Mose explained briefly, then straightened his back and turned to face the door, just as two grunts came in.

Caspian's arm pulled me close into him, and we crouched and listened quietly.

"It's your turn today, Mose," one of the daemons said, his voice rough and low. I'd only caught a glimpse of them, but I'd registered their impressive height and size. They made the hut look tiny.

"No way to avoid this any longer," the other added.

We heard Mose clear his throat as he shuffled toward the exit.

"I hear you, I hear you," he replied, cursing under his breath.

"It won't take longer than a couple of hours," the first daemon grumbled.

"Unless they catch you lying." The other scoffed as all three left the hut.

We waited for a couple of minutes, and I used my True Sight to watch as the daemons escorted Mose up an alley leading toward the city center, where the giant tower stood, surrounded by palace walls.

"What the hell?" I gasped, staring at Caspian.

"I'm just as in the dark as you are," he replied, as we emerged from our hiding spot. "He's supposed to have good standing in the city. On one hand because of his role as a cleric, but also because he helps around the city. Shaytan looks favorably upon elders with a... sense of civic duty."

"At least we learned a new trick with the ashes," Caia replied, dusting herself off.

"What do we do now?" I asked, checking the areas outside the hut. Barely a handful of daemons were around, all of them old, weak, and barely moving, supporting their weight on gnarled wooden canes.

"We should wait here for Mose to come back," Caspian replied. "You heard the grunts. I doubt Mose will willingly get himself in trouble here. Besides, this place gives us a good vantage point."

He moved toward one of the two small, circular windows I hadn't seen before, hidden beneath a layer of black cloth. He slowly lifted the fabric to peek outside.

"Do you think he'll be back? I mean, do you think they'll let him go?" I murmured, not feeling too optimistic in a city as savage as this.

"I don't know." Caspian sighed, his shoulders dropping. "But if he doesn't, we can keep moving in a couple of hours. We can devise a plan, and I can show you a few more useful parts of the city, in case Mose doesn't return. He is right. I must go on, with or without him..."

I found myself in awe of Caspian. So many secrets concealed behind those jade eyes. Such a strong sense of duty and such a desire to help the innocent... and yet he wasn't actively working with his own species on this.

I was intrigued and filled with even more questions, but at least we'd learned something about the daemons. Most importantly, we'd learned that Fiona's abductor, Zane, was one of the Seven Princes, and a son of the king of daemons. I didn't have time to properly digest that particular nugget, given the sudden arrival of those grunts, but whoa...

Fiona had been abducted, then released by a prince of daemons. What had been his end game? What was he hoping to achieve with that? I wished I could simply call Fiona, or use Telluris to tell her, but... that was obviously out of the question.

Besides, I had a feeling that by the time we saw each other again, I'd have a lot more to tell her about this city and its evil, soul-eating inhabitants...

24

FIONA

(DAUGHTER OF BENEDICT & YELENA)

It felt like a dream. The moment in which Zane blew yellow dust in my face was played on a loop. My eyes popped open, the utter darkness replaced by faint shapes against the streetlamps outside, their lights fluttering amber in the night. I sat up with a gasp, my muscles hard and tense. I'd expected to wake up in a cage, in a cave buried deep in the gorges again.

I breathed a sigh of relief once I realized I was still in the bookstore. Also, I'd been put in one of the armchairs in the reading corner.

What the hell was Zane thinking?

I went over my last conversation with him, trying to pick up on any details that might come in handy later. Something told me I'd see him again, and I was determined not to get fooled by that damn yellow powder next time.

After a couple of minutes of processing everything that had just happened, I left the bookstore and went back to my room at the Broken Bow Inn. There was a square white giftbox waiting for me outside my door, with an elegant pale green organza ribbon and a note from Vincent.

I saw this and thought of you. I look forward to seeing you tonight. Yours always, Vincent.

My cheeks caught fire. I still wasn't used to that kind of attention, but I had to admit, it felt nice to be pampered like that once in a while. Given the mess we'd gotten ourselves into with this whole Neraka business, I could at least enjoy the few spare moments I had between running for my life and killing daemons coming for my soul.

I went into my room and opened the box. A gorgeous dress awaited, layer upon layer of delicate, ivory-colored organza with thousands of perfect pearls, along with matching earrings and a pair of elegant shoes.

A smile settled on my face, and I lifted the dress in the air, loving how the light threw shimmering reflections at it from all angles. I slipped into the shower, then got ready for my dinner with Vincent, all the while going over my encounter with Zane —repeatedly, almost obsessively. I kept looking for something that wasn't there, eager to replay the scene in which he'd pushed me against the wall and hidden his face in my hair.

My skin tingled as I put the dress on, pulling the fine long sleeves over my arms. I wasn't sure whether it was the fabric or the memory of Zane's touch that had such an effect on me. A couple of deep breaths later, I stepped into the shoes, and took a gander at myself in the mirror.

Why am I still thinking about him? What the hell is wrong with me?

I shook my head, then put the pearl earrings on, sprinkled a little perfume from the small fragrance atomizer I'd brought from The Shade, and stilled. A chill trickled through my limbs —I found myself under the impression that someone was watching.

Was I getting paranoid, or was there a daemon around? I carefully scanned the room, but the air seemed normal, and there wasn't a single glimmer of red eyes. *No, I'm just imagining it.*

Not that I could be blamed for feeling on edge, based on what had happened earlier.

I left my room, blowing out the lights on my way out, and locked the door behind me. There was tension mounting in the air around me, but it was all part of my thought process. I was feeling watched, followed, and constantly surveyed.

Spotting Zane at the bookstore had kicked off alarm signals in my head. I was seeing him everywhere, so to speak. Whenever I found myself alone now, I couldn't help but look over my shoulder and check... just in case.

The daemons had definitely played a part in this... trauma, for lack of a better word. I'd never been this guarded before. It took daemons using invisibility spells to try to kill us in order for me to become more aware of my surroundings.

But it felt as though I were taking this state of alertness just one step too far. There was no daemon following me. I was on my own as I walked up the alley leading to the White Star Hotel.

Surprisingly enough, I was hoping I'd see Zane again sooner rather than later, though I didn't know why, exactly.

I must be losing my mind...

25

AVRIL

(DAUGHTER OF LUCAS & MARION)

Lemuel's studio on the first level could easily be described as a dump. It was a large room, tucked away on the first floor of what looked like a derelict building in the slums of Azure Heights. His choice of location actually made sense, as few to none would think of looking around these parts for... anything, really.

He locked the door behind him, then walked across the room, which was filled with old furniture covered in dirty cotton sheets. There was a wooden bookshelf leaning against the wall at the end, loaded with dusty books, and a lever hidden behind an encyclopedia. The old Iman pressed it, and the entire bookshelf shuddered, clouds of dust falling off in thick rolls as he pushed it to the side.

Heron and I were speechless at the sight of a small, hidden

chamber filled with boxes of scrolls and manuscripts, their pages yellowed by the passage of time.

"I keep everything here," Lemuel grumbled as he started looking through the scrolls, selecting a handful, which he handed over. "I don't know why, but I just do. It's like... something inside me tells me that I need to preserve the history of my people and keep it away from the Maras... so, I do."

"Yeah, you've been mind-bent like crazy." Heron frowned, staring at the old Iman.

Lemuel blinked several times, then shrugged, while we started reading through the scrolls he gave us.

"That's highly probable, and I don't know why. But as long as they don't know about the archives, I'm good. They can't make me forget about something they don't even know I have, right?"

"Fair point," I muttered, while scanning the texts.

"It says here that there was a hundred-year war between the Maras and the Imen when the Maras first arrived on Neraka," Heron said, checking another scroll. "But there is no mention of a truce. I specifically remember the Lords telling us about a truce, about how they came to finally get along with the Imen, when they swore an oath to only consume animal blood and so on..."

"I don't know what to tell you," Lemuel replied. "All I know is that there is a long-standing truce, but I have no idea who signed it, or when it took place. It's just common knowledge. Something we've learned since we were children."

"Do you remember anyone teaching you that, in particular?" I asked, suspecting another instance of the Maras mind-bending "facts" into the Imen's heads.

Lemuel shook his head, then gave me a large notebook filled with handwritten notes and sketches. I recognized the daemons in the drawings, but not all of the creatures. Some of the illustrations were quite strange, depicting massive beasts, along with pit wolves and what looked like giant bats with big, round red eyes. The artist had used red ink to emphasize that specific trait.

I started reading entire passages from the notebook, instinctively looking at Heron whenever fact and fiction met in the middle.

"Heron," I muttered, "this is supposed to be a collection of myths and legends…"

"And the truth seems stranger than fiction?" He sighed, giving me a faint smile, while Lemuel kept scouring his archives for anything we could use regarding the daemons.

"No, that's the thing. This is supposed to be fiction, but everything I've read so far is real… what the daemons look like, what they feed on, where they hunt," I replied. "Even their underground cities and their use of magic, which the Imen identify as 'foreign power'."

Heron frowned, then moved closer to me so he could read, too. His eyes wandered across the pieces of text for a while.

"I see they mention the armored daemons here… the hierarchy in their cities, along with Seven Princes and a King Shaytan," he breathed, then looked up at Lemuel. "Lemuel, is all this meant to be lore?"

The old Iman stopped his search and straightened his back, groaning from physical discomfort.

"Yes, just... just ancient mythology, at least two thousand years old. Tales passed on from one generation to another, scribbled down by the few Imen left behind in Azure City who could write," he replied, taking a seat on a nearby stool. Its wooden legs creaked under his weight.

"A lot of the stuff in these scrolls and books is true, though," Heron said. "At least, as far as we've seen, in the Valley of Screams."

Lemuel thought about it for a second, then put on a half-smile.

"Don't tell the other Imen, then." He sighed. "It's bad enough they're being taken away by these invisible beasts. If you tell them they're organized and whatnot, it'll scare them to death."

"Tell me something, Lemuel," I asked. "How come there is so little written history of your people?"

"Well, it all goes back to the founding of Azure Heights," the old Iman replied, scratching the back of his head. "The majority of Imen in the region chose to live beyond the gorges, away from the Maras' new city. At the time, there were millions of Imen inhabiting the planet, so we didn't think much of the newcomers settling on the mountain. Those of us left behind, however, didn't know how to read or write—most of us, anyway.

There were a couple of scholars among us. We went into servi-
tude and learned to coexist with the Maras, while the rest of our
people died out in the world."

"But why? How do millions just die out?" I frowned, unable
to wrap my head around the mysterious demise of nearly an
entire species. "The daemons ate their souls, or what?"

"That's what the lore says, yes." Lemuel nodded slowly,
sadness pulling the corners of his mouth down. "I've only been
around for some decades, milady. All I have to work with are
these pieces of paper, as far as the past of my people goes... and
it's mostly legends and tales. I'm afraid I don't know anything
else beyond that."

There were still many unanswered questions weighing
down on us, but at least we were getting somewhere with all
these searches. We were getting *some* answers, even though each
left the door open to more unknowns.

"There's one thing we know for a fact," Heron said, his eyes
fixed on me, as if he'd just read my mind. "The Maras are mind-
bending the Imen on a much broader scale than they've
told us."

"Which means they lied to us," I concluded, my stomach
turning.

"Our most burning question is why." He raised an eyebrow.
"But we need to find a way to ask it without arousing suspicion.
Who do we talk to about this?"

"My money's on Arrah. Once she takes her brother to safety,
I'm sure she'll be able to shed some light on the matter."

Heron nodded, then briefly glanced at Lemuel before shifting his intense focus back to me.

"I think we should try another exploratory mission once Harper and the others are back," he said, a playful twinkle settling in his pale green eyes. "We could find the tribes beyond the gorges and hear what *they* have to say about all this."

"You know what?" I replied with a smirk. "For a guy who prides himself on, and I quote, 'not liking the overly brainy stuff much', your words, not mine... you're a pretty smart cookie."

"You're rubbing off on me, that's all." Heron gave me a warm smile, lighting me up on the inside. I couldn't help but return it, feeling my lips stretch and my heart sing. Even our banter was taking on a sweet tone, and... I loved it.

"Are you two married?" the old Iman asked, his question crashing into me like a bucket of icy water. I nearly broke into a sweat trying to answer that. *Why am I having trouble answering that?*

Heron and I stared at him for a couple of seconds, then looked at each other and almost simultaneously cleared our throats.

"No, we're not," Heron replied. "We're part of the same team, and that's it—"

"Oh, please!" Lemuel gave us a dismissive wave of his hand. "The longer you deny it, the faster you two are going to burn. My wife and I did the same and wasted ten years before we got together. Both of us were too proud to take the first step, and... well, that's a decade we could have spent loving each other."

What do you say to that?

I was already burning on the inside. Judging by the look on Heron's face, so was he. But were we ablaze because of the dynamic between us, or because Lemuel had seen through us in ways I'd never thought possible?

So, on top of all the questions we had about the Imen, the Exiled Maras, and the daemons, Heron and I were facing ourselves under a big fat question mark. What were we to each other? Most importantly, what did I want him to be to me?

I am in so much trouble...

26

SCARLETT

(DAUGHTER OF JERAMIAH & PIPPA)

We made it down to the first level of the city, and spent about half an hour looking for Master Specter's store. This part of Azure Heights was a bit more complicated as far as the streets were concerned—there were no straight lines, but plenty of sinuous junctions, making it easy to miss a turn along the way.

Master Specter's shop could easily be missed, given the rustic appearance of the building that housed it. We were on the less "slummy" side of town, but the level of poverty was still visible to the naked eye. Most of the Imen moving around were covered in tattered dark gray and brown cloaks, and some could do with new pairs of shoes.

The store was closed—the shutters were down, and the main door was locked.

"He closed already?" Patrik muttered, looking around the corner for any sign of life.

"It looks like it," I replied, gazing at the hand-painted sign hung over the door. *Specter's Shop* was written in beautiful cursive, with elegant swirls and floral embellishments. "I guess we'll have to wait until tomorrow for the fair."

"I was hoping we'd cover more ground by then, but—"

"What do you want?" An old man's throaty voice reverberated from above, interrupting Patrik.

We both glanced up and saw an Iman in his mid-seventies glaring down at us. His skin was pale, and his long white hair was braided in a pattern similar to that of his beard. Metallic beads capped each braid, and they jingled slightly whenever he moved.

"Are you Master Specter?" Patrik asked.

"Who are you?"

"I'm Patrik, and this is Scarlett. We're part of the team that came to help you with your daemon problem."

"Ah, yes... I remember you." The old Iman nodded, with a glimmer of recognition in his pale blue eyes. "You came here in a big ball of light."

"Indeed." Patrik nodded, then frowned. "I thought those bearing the Master titles were all Maras. Or am I wrong?"

"You *are* wrong. Though there are very few of my kind who qualify for the title," Master Specter replied. "Not many literate Imen left in this city, since our people moved out to the western plains. My family line held true to its tradition. Writing and reading were skills that my forefathers did not wish to see fade away with the passage of time."

"I understand. We're here because we were told you might be able to help us with some ingredients," Patrik said.

"What are you looking for? I trade in many things."

"Herbs and crystals that the Maras might have brought over here from Calliope. Fire orchids, green apatite, and Zurian garnet, to be precise."

The old Iman thought about it for a minute, scratching his chin through his beard.

"I don't have any of those, but come to the fair tomorrow," he replied. "I know someone who sells the orchids and the apatite, but you won't find him anywhere at this time of night. He's a peculiar fellow..."

I exhaled sharply, somewhat disappointed that we still had to wait until the morning. Master Specter noticed my dismay, and gave us a brief smile.

"You're not going to find Zurian garnet anywhere, though," he continued. "The few stones that the Maras brought over from their world are currently set in ancient jewelry now. But Neraka has plenty of its own resources. They may not have an identical composition, but they'll come close enough. There is a garnet mine on the north side, at the base of the mountain. Its walls are riddled with red garnet. The Maras use it for jewelry. You could try that. Take the main road out of the city and turn right at the golden poles. The mine will be about half a mile farther, covered in red flowers."

Patrik and I looked at each other, then shrugged in agreement. It was worth a shot.

"Thank you, Master Specter," Patrik said, and bowed curtly.

"Yes, yes, you're welcome and whatnot." The old Iman waved him away. "But don't go out there at night. That area is riddled with dangers. It's why we stopped mining after dark."

"Dangers... You mean daemons?" I asked, and he nodded. "Not to worry, we'll be careful. Thank you!"

"Don't say I didn't warn you," he muttered, then pulled the shutters tight and closed his windows. My blood ran cold with the thought of running into more daemons, but, after what we'd been through in the Valley of Screams, the prospect didn't seem that frightening anymore. I knew what they looked like and what they were capable of.

It's easier to fight an enemy you know.

"Let's go," Patrik said, walking toward the main road leading down to the plain.

I followed, still replaying the kiss in my mind. The silence between us was something I'd sort of expected. My mind was blank, as I was still adjusting to a reality in which Patrik and I had kissed. Somewhere deep down, fear of rejection lingered— fear that Patrik would later turn around and tell me never to do that again. On the other hand, he had said that he could "see" me. That he acknowledged me as more than just a teammate.

And here I go, overthinking things at the wrong time...

The night sky above had turned indigo, with passing clouds that swallowed the stars as they moved toward the east. The second moon was coming up in shades of amber, casting a warmer light over the jagged edges and corners of the city's white buildings, the picket fences, and the brown cobblestones beneath our feet.

I stayed behind Patrik for a while, just taking a few minutes to admire his entire frame, from the messy and curly black hair that inched longer at the back, to his broad shoulders and narrow hips—perfectly framed by his black pants and white cotton shirt, fitted with belts and straps to keep his fighting equipment and Druid supplies in place. I didn't even notice him stop until I bumped into him.

"I... Sorry, Patrik, I... I wasn't looking," I mumbled, then moved around and proceeded to walk by his side. He watched me quietly as we headed down the main road, occasionally glancing over his shoulder.

"Are you okay?" he asked, his voice softer than usual.

"Of course. All good, nothing to worry about." I forced my face into a smile that felt more like a plastic grin.

"Worried about what might wait for us down at the mine?" His blue eyes nearly pierced through my soul, leaving me with a feeling of nakedness and vulnerability that I had no idea how to overcome. I gave him a weak nod in response, hoping that would end our conversation.

I was getting nervous, mostly because I wanted him to talk about the kiss—I was dying to hear his thoughts, and, at the same time, I was terrified, but it wasn't the right time, and I saw no point in just filling the silence with other words. Every thought that my mind was producing was leading back to our kiss in the library.

Thankfully, he didn't say much else, either, until we reached the mine.

We both stopped to stare at it for a couple of minutes. It was just as Master Specter had described it, but it looked absolutely stunning. The garnet mine had a diamond-shaped entrance, with red light flickering from inside, confirming the rich crystal deposits within. It was sheltered beneath a sharp ridge, covered in a sea of red flowers that reminded me of poppies, with large, square petals and thin stems. It contrasted beautifully against the tall, green grass of the plain behind us, and the patches of gray limestone of the mountain base.

"I think it's best if I go in, and you keep a lookout," Patrik suggested.

I opened my mouth to reply, but froze as the air rippled just a couple of feet behind him.

"Patrik, watch out!" I growled, and immediately took my sword out, my gaze locked on a pair of red, glimmering eyes as I rushed toward the daemon.

Patrik muttered a spell under his breath, and I heard water splashing, just as I ran my sword through an invisible daemon's throat. Droplets of water reached us, some trickling down the fiend's face and revealing him, inch by inch, as he gurgled blood.

The screech of a sword was followed by heavy grunting. I turned around and was swiftly faced by another, now-visible daemon. There were two of them left, and Patrik was fighting the other one.

I dodged my second opponent's long claws—he missed my side by an inch, at most, further riling me up. He was about five times my size, as far as muscle mass was concerned, and held at least another foot over me. He was quite agile, repeatedly coming at me with his bare hands, but he wasn't as fast as "the Bullet".

I swerved to the left and rammed my fist into his ribs, then darted to the right just as he turned to hit me. I brought my sword up in a diagonal movement and caught his chest in full, the blade sinking at least four inches into his flesh before coming back out with a blood spurt.

He groaned from the pain, and I quickly turned and beheaded him before he could think of retaliation. The horned bastard hadn't stood a chance, and, judging by the collapsed mess in front of Patrik, the third daemon hadn't made it either.

Patrik and I exchanged glances. He gave me a wink and a confident smirk, then sheathed his sword. He froze, staring somewhere behind me, and gripped his sword again. My instincts kicked in again, and I turned to see two more daemons, both invisible and rippling through the air above us as they jumped off the ridge.

Before I could even bring my sword up, however, a large black mass shot from the bushes behind the ridge and rammed into one of the daemons. Patrik took on the other one, jumping in front of me, his sword coming out of its scabbard once more.

"What the…" I managed, as Patrik killed his opponent in less than a minute and looked for the black mass. I found it just twenty feet from us and stilled, realizing what I was looking at. "Patrik, the pit wolf…"

The giant, black-skinned creature with large red eyes had its fangs sunk into an invisible daemon's throat, judging by the shape forming beneath a coat of fresh, jugular blood.

"Whoa," I murmured, as the pit wolf shuddered and tossed the daemon aside like an old rag doll. "That's a… good boy?"

Patrik moved in front of me, in an attempt to shield me from whatever the pit wolf might do next, but I put my hand on his shoulder and squeezed gently, unable to take my eyes off the creature.

"Don't," I said to Patrik, recognizing the pit wolf without a charmed collar. "It's the one we sort of rescued. He won't hurt us. I think…"

The beast licked its furless snout, its tongue dangling loosely to the side, and came closer. I walked toward it, putting my sword away and extending my arms out in a peaceful gesture—my heart was hammering in my chest, but I had faith I'd live through this encounter.

The pit wolf huffed, then shook its immense head and sat on all fours, like a giant dog. Its eyes were gentle as it waited for me to approach it.

"Scarlett, please, be careful," Patrik muttered behind me. I knew he was ready to intervene if needed, so that gave me the extra ounce of courage I needed to reach the creature.

"It's okay," I said softly, addressing both Patrik and my strange new ally. "I won't hurt you... and I'm guessing you don't want to hurt me either?"

The pit wolf put its head down on the ground, patiently waiting for me to make the next move. I touched its nose with one trembling hand. It was cold and wet. *Just like a dog. Hah...*

I stroked the top of its head as gently as possible, and it responded with a low growl, as if it enjoyed my touch. It made me smile as I looked in its eyes—two pools of red that yielded nothing but gratitude and affection.

"I think we're okay here, Patrik," I said. "You should go inside and take what you need from the mine. Wolf-thingy here and I will keep an eye out for other hunter daemons."

"Just... be careful," Patrik replied, and climbed into the mine.

I continued stroking the pit wolf's head. It licked my arm, then slipped forward and slapped its pink tongue against my face, making me giggle and nearly lose my footing. I then moved to scratch its back, focusing on the bony area of its shoulder blades.

"Hah, you like that, don't you?" I muttered, delighted by the creature's reaction. It rolled onto its back, blatantly demanding a belly rub. "You've got to be kidding me..."

The pit wolf lay there, its tongue out, waiting.

"Okay, fine, a belly rub it is, then." I chuckled and scratched its belly. The skin was soft and warm, a shade of black so intense it seemed unreal, as if someone had painted this creature with black ink. "I should give you a name, though... don't you think?"

It yawned, stretching lazily, enjoying the belly rub. My arm was getting tired—this was one big animal to pet! *And... a male. Okay...* As if sensing my intention to withdraw my hand, *he* sat up on *his* hind legs, then brought his head down and nuzzled my face.

"You are ridiculously friendly, dude! I like you!" I smiled, stroking his thick, muscular neck. He was roughly shorter than an Asian elephant, at a little over two meters, and made me feel so small, yet his ability to exude so much affection made me think of him as a gentle giant. "I'll bet those collars make you mean, but you're not mean by nature, are you?"

The pit wolf huffed again, as if understanding what I'd just asked, and slowly shook his head as he stared at me. A thought crossed my mind then.

"Do you understand what I'm saying?"

He didn't take his eyes off me, but didn't react, either. *Maybe I'm overestimating his abilities...*

"Can I call you Jack?"

He blinked a couple of times, then nodded once. *Oh, hell...*

"I don't know why, but I think Jack suits you." I shrugged, watching his expression carefully for any sign that he could, in fact, understand me. "Jack is the name of a guy I know back in my world. He lives in Hawaii. It's a beautiful island; you'd love it. Anyway, Jack is a human. A big one. He's like... a gentle giant. Kind of like you."

I heard Patrik inside the mine—a metal pick hitting a hard wall, scraping and crumbling sounds followed by another clang. Both Jack and I looked around, checking for hostiles nearby. We seemed to be in the clear for the time being.

"I don't understand why you're here, though," I said to the pit wolf. He nuzzled my face again, licking my ear in the process. "Is it because I released you from that collar, maybe?"

He groaned and hid his face against my chest, knocking me over. I laughed and got up, gently stroking his back.

"It's okay now, Jack," I murmured. "I promise I'll do the same with every pit wolf I see out there. It's not fair that they use you like that. You must have been so miserable..."

A couple of minutes went by as I replayed the scene from earlier in my head. Jack had known exactly where to jump and what to bite into in order to deliver a deadly blow.

"Jack, can you see the daemons?" I asked, though I wasn't sure I'd get an answer. The pit wolf seemed selective in his responses. Jack let out a long and low growl. "I'm not sure what to make of that answer, but I'll just assume it's a yes, for now. Or that at least your senses are sharp. Really sharp."

Patrik emerged from the cave with a handful of red garnet crystals. He handed them over, and I shoved them into my backpack, while he stared at the pit wolf. Jack held his ground, but seemed to accept Patrik near him... and me. Which was good. The last thing I needed was a repeat of our kiss at some point in the near future, and Jack jumping out of nowhere, biting Patrik's face off...

"Is it friendly?" Patrik smirked, slowly reaching a hand out.

"*He* hasn't eaten me yet," I replied, patting the pit wolf's head. "I named him Jack. It's a he. I saw... *them*."

Patrik laughed lightly as Jack licked his hand.

"He definitely likes you," he replied, watching with slight amusement as Jack lifted his massive weight back onto all fours, towering over me while sniffing and slobbering over the entire right side of my face. How could I push this massive lump of love away? I was head over heels already!

We walked back toward the city, moving through the tall grass. Jack stayed by my side, constantly looking around and sniffing the air. Once we reached the main road, however, the pit wolf wavered and yelped, shaking his head.

I looked at Patrik, then patted Jack's back as he sat on his hind legs.

"I think it's best if you stay out of sight, buddy," I said gently. "The Maras, the Imen, they don't know you like we do... They will get scared and try to hurt you. Stay in the shadows, okay, Jack?"

As if understanding everything I'd just said, the pit wolf licked my face one more time, then shuffled through the grass until he disappeared behind a thick layer of shrubs climbing up the mountainside.

Patrik and I returned to the main road, heading back to the Broken Bow Inn. We'd done everything we could for one day. The rest of our mission revolved around the Spring Fair, opening the next day.

I occasionally glanced over my shoulder and caught flickers of Jack's red eyes in the dark woods beneath. This time it wasn't a feeling—I knew for a fact that I'd see him again, and soon.

27

HARPER

(DAUGHTER OF HAZEL & TEJUS)

Several hours passed as we waited in Mose's hut, but there was no sign of him. I kept scanning the area, watching daemons as they moved around, but I couldn't see Mose anywhere.

"What if he's not coming back?" I asked, breaking the silence that had settled over us for about ten minutes. "What if they've detained him? Has he told you anything about why they might come looking for him in the first place, Lord Kifo?"

"No, and that's what bothers me the most," Caspian replied, leaning against the wall as he peeked through the window. "He is leading an underground resistance, of sorts, but they can't possibly trace it back to him. He's been extremely careful until now... I don't get it."

"A resistance?" Jax frowned, still sitting next to Hansa by the small firepit in the middle. "A resistance against what?"

"Against King Shaytan," Caspian explained. "Believe it or not, there are plenty of daemons out there who don't agree with this... lifestyle of theirs. They're not all monsters."

"No, only the ones in charge." I scoffed, shaking my head slowly.

"Daemons are not born evil, Miss Hellswan." Caspian's jade gaze pierced through me like an intense laser beam. "They are made evil by the system in which they've been raised. However, there are daemons who reject the doctrine, who refuse to hurt other creatures. But soul eating is a powerful tool that the king uses to enslave his own people. All it takes is one taste, and that's it. It becomes nearly impossible to break free. You have to feed again. And again. And again. The hunger manifests in the form of excruciating pain, and it takes a lot of strength and support from others in order to break free. And what support can these creatures get from a society that is convinced there's no other way besides eating souls in the first place?"

"You talk as if you've experienced this firsthand," I muttered, watching the colors around him change to a deep red with waves of dark gray. Something bothered him. I'd struck a nerve.

"I've seen the effects of it. I've seen what it looks like when the soul courses through your veins, and I've seen what it does to your body once you deprive it of such powerful energy," Caspian replied, shifting his gaze to what lay beyond the window.

"What do we do, though?" Blaze interjected, while Caia played with the flames in the pit, her fingers moving as she raised little swirls of fire from the pile of burning wood. "We can't just stay here forever..."

"I agree, we should go out." I nodded. "Maybe check their military resources... their prison... They must have one."

"They most certainly do," Caspian replied, then straightened his back as he saw something outside, something worthy of his full attention. "Wait. There's movement in the main square. They're all rushing to it..."

I used my True Sight, confirming what Caspian had just observed. Daemons of all shapes and sizes were pouring down the alleys leading into the city center, where the palace and giant tower awaited.

"Should we go see what that's about?" I asked Jax and Hansa, who noticed the enthusiasm in my voice.

"You sound excited." Hansa raised an eyebrow.

"More like bored." I shrugged. "I'm tired of waiting around."

"Let's go," Jax replied, then stood up. "But we'll have to use the invisibility spell. We can't risk being in the middle of a daemon crowd without it."

Hansa, Blaze, and Caia sprang to their feet, and Jax dispensed portions of what was left of our invisibility spell paste. We had to swipe some from hunter daemons the first chance we got, if we wanted to leave the underground city without letting the dragon loose and getting into a fight we may not be able to win.

We swallowed the paste and held hands, waiting for the spell to kick in. Caspian took one of my hands, while Hansa held onto the other, with Jax, Caia, and Blaze following closely. We left the hut and snuck through the narrow streets leading into the city, staying close to the walls to avoid the engorging crowd, and occasionally hiding in various nooks and side alleys to calculate our next steps.

The king's palace towered over us, its shiny black walls reflecting the amber flames burning below. We were less than fifty yards from a massive swarm of daemons that had gathered outside the palace steps, where armed guards had lined up— about twenty of them at the base and another twenty at the top of the stairs.

"I think it's best if we get as close to those stairs as possible," Jax whispered, as we watched more daemons joining the others in the main square.

We had a good viewing angle from our spot. I could see a large, rectangular space in front of the palace stairs, lined by servants, who kept the rest of the crowd at bay.

"Got it," I replied. Caspian squeezed my hand tighter.

He guided me back out into the main street, and the others followed. We walked on the edge toward the gathering. We reached the main square and slipped through the crowd, and Caspian got us closer to the palace steps. We came to a halt at the sound of massive drums beating somewhere behind the upper line of armed guards. The rhythm was solid and intense, each thud loud enough to send shivers down my spine. The daemons growled and roared around us.

They all grinned, excited and restless as they waited for something.

"Fall back," a daemon shouted, his voice echoing across the square.

The armed guards at the top obeyed and split into two groups, leaving room in the middle of the platform for a group of six large daemons to come through. They resembled each other, as far as facial features were concerned, and were uniformly dressed in black leather, with fur coats hanging loosely on their shoulders. They carried bejeweled broadswords on their gold belts, and gold threads were woven on their twisted horns.

Royalty of some kind...

"All hail the Six Princes!" the same voice announced. I used my True Sight to scan the area and found the drummers, along with a daemon dressed in dark red, somewhere behind the giant columns framing the main entrance into the palace.

"Wait, six? I thought there were seven," I whispered. There were several feet of space around us, and the crowd was far too loud for anyone to hear me.

"There *are* seven princes. I guess one of them isn't here," Caspian breathed, then shushed me, pulling me closer. I could feel the warmth of his body seeping into mine. I kept myself glued to him, watching the scene at the top of the palace stairs unfold before us.

The princes nodded, and the commoners and the crowd erupted in cheers and whistles. Judging by their reactions, the king's sons were quite popular. But not as popular as the king himself, I noted, as silence fell heavy over the square.

King Shaytan emerged from the palace, and roars of adoration and worship exploded from every single daemon around us. I could see it on their faces—the broad smiles, the flaming red eyes, and the feverish hand gestures. Whatever the king said, they gobbled it up. It didn't come as much of a surprise, though. The guy was... huge. King Shaytan was bigger than all the other daemons I'd seen so far, including the massive ones lugging Imen cages around. His skin carried a bronze tan, his muscles perfectly sculpted on his enormous frame. He wore golden chainmail around his waist, snugly strapped with a bejeweled belt just below his narrow hips. A giant piece of animal fur rested on his back, a thick gold chain keeping it over his shoulder—whatever animal it had belonged to, it was either extremely rare or even extinct, as I'd never seen that zebra-like pattern anywhere else. The black and white contrast definitely made him stand out, though...

A sturdy and beautifully crafted gold crown rested on his head; his long salt-and-pepper hair was braided into thick dreadlocks, sewn with gold thread, and caught with a thick gold bangle at the back. His horns were significantly longer and thicker than the others', twisting twice as they curved downward, nearly reaching his buttocks. He held a long, slim staff made entirely out of gold, with a large, oval red garnet crystal mounted at the top. It looked as though two golden claws swirled around it. It had a peculiar glimmer, amplified by the fires burning in copper wall sconces behind him.

His arms, his chest, and his abdomen were covered in black tattoos, a myriad of geometric symbols displayed in vertical rows, dancing over the ropes of muscle with every move he made. I gripped Caspian's arm tighter, my fingers digging into his flesh; he returned the gesture by wrapping his spare arm around me. I was genuinely scared at the sight of the daemon king—and with good reason, too.

He was, by far, the strongest I had ever seen of his kind, and his people adored and obeyed him. *We are in so much freakin' trouble...*

King Shaytan raised his arms slowly, prompting the crowd to go quiet all of a sudden.

"For too long have we kept to the underground," he spoke, his voice low and downright seductive. No wonder he had no trouble getting new wives every year! "For too long, we've allowed others to consume the souls that are rightfully ours."

The crowd went wild, cheering him on, before he raised his hands again to demand silence—they sealed their lips shut in response.

"Rightfully ours? Seriously?" I whispered, mostly to myself. Caspian squeezed my shoulder, reminding me to keep quiet.

I lifted my head to get a better look, and noticed a large, empty space at the bottom of the stairs. King Shaytan clapped his hands once, and the ground started shaking beneath us. My blood froze as I used my True Sight and spotted the source of that instantaneous mini-earthquake. About a thousand large daemons marched from the side, filling the space I'd just seen in front of the palace stairs.

They were massive grunts, clad in heavy armor and carrying shields, spears, and broad rapiers with ivory handles. They came to a halt in the middle, then turned to face the crowd, their faces seemingly carved from stone.

"For too long have we allowed those bloodsuckers up there to keep us from thriving as we should," King Shaytan continued, his voice booming across the square. "And now, they have the audacity to call their friends from whatever dirty rock they came from in the first place! It is time we teach them a lesson. Last night's... fireworks were just a taste of what's to come!"

Fireworks... Oh, wow, that's how he's chosen to refer to the explosions that claimed the lives of dozens of innocent Imen and Maras. I was disgusted, my stomach churning.

Servant daemons moved through the newly formed garrison, checking that their breastplates and large cuffs were mounted properly, occasionally tugging at and tying loose strings. Others carried wicker baskets around, from which they handed out small leather pouches to each grunt. I had a feeling those were invisibility spell supplies.

"Tonight, my dear subjects," King Shaytan grinned, his red eyes beaming as he scanned the crowd, "tonight we teach those newcomers not to underestimate our glorious species anymore! Soldiers!"

The grunts let out a collective roar, then turned to face their king. The crowd around us grew restless, unable to take their eyes off Shaytan. Their adulation was starting to creep me out.

"Go into Azure Heights, and bring me those newcomers," the king ordered, and the grunts nodded. "Bring them alive. All of them. Especially the dragon. I need a new pet, anyway..."

The air left my lungs. Ice poured through my veins as I instinctively started looking around me—I couldn't see Blaze standing next to us, of course, though he was there. Several scenarios started rumbling through my head, but none ended with any of us walking out of this mess alive.

The king of daemons was about to send an army after us. The entire city of Azure Heights was vulnerable. Half of us were in here already, while Scarlett, Patrik, Avril, Hansa, and Fiona were back there.

We have to do something... We can't let the daemon army go.

We're... We're so screwed...

28

CAIA

(DAUGHTER OF GRACE & LAWRENCE)

I froze, holding Blaze's hand tightly as the king of daemons announced to his crowd that he wanted our dragon as a... pet. I was disgusted and terrified at the same time. Blaze seemed to feel my distress somehow, as he pulled me closer, his hot breath warming the top of my head. I felt so tiny and helpless in our position.

"What do we do?" I whispered.

"What *can* we do?" Hansa breathed. "There are too many of them. We're in the middle of their city!"

"We can't let them go out," Harper interjected, her voice trembling. "We have to stop them..."

The king continued his speech, addressing his soldiers, who got louder and more aggressive with every minute that went by, stomping their feet and beating their chests, and the crowd around us got even more restless.

"For too long, we've kept to our cities and allowed the Maras to thrive," King Shaytan growled. "It's time we take our world back. We are the rightful rulers. The strongest. The undefeated."

My stomach shrank to the size of a pea. We really had no other choice at this point, and very little time to figure out a strategy to both prevent the army from reaching the city and not get ourselves killed.

"We have to reveal ourselves," Harper sighed. "Draw attention to the fact that we're here... We have to get their minds off invading Azure Heights..."

"I just need to get to a high altitude point and go dragon on these monsters, while they're all gathered in one place. It's better if I do it from somewhere above than from the ground, where they might try to poke my eyes out," Blaze whispered. "You don't need to reveal yourselves for this."

A couple of seconds went by. Shaytan kept agitating his subjects, raising goosebumps all over my skin. The savagery, the hunger, and the desire to hurt others was downright terrifying.

"No, we have to show ourselves. They need to see us down here so they don't think we just sent the dragon to roast them. It's essential that we keep the daemons focused on *us* and not Azure Heights. We'll reveal ourselves and give you the window you need to get to a good spot. The tower," Harper replied. "Get to the top of the tower and douse them with as much fire as your giant lungs can produce, Blaze."

"I don't think I can cover the whole city, though. My flames don't have such a broad range. But I can definitely take on the square. You'll have angry daemons down in the streets afterward," he breathed, thinking out loud, while the daemons around us stomped their feet, agreeing to whatever else Shaytan had just said.

"It'll be good enough," Caspian intervened. "As long as you burn this whole damn square to the ground, it'll give us the chance to spread out and head for the tunnel from whence we came. We won't need a live daemon to get back through the cloaking spell, so we'll just run out."

"I'm guessing no one ever escapes a city of daemons, so there was no point in sticking to the original cloaking spell?" Harper replied.

"More or less, yes," Caspian replied. "I think it has more to do with the daemons using slightly different ingredients, as opposed to the original swamp witch formula."

"So what do we do once we get back to the surface?" I asked, my whole body trembling from the mounting tension around us.

"Let's get to the surface first," Jax murmured.

I wasn't one to scare easily, but this whole situation was starting to get to me. We were grossly outnumbered, and even outgunned, with just one dragon against thousands of swamp witch magic-wielding daemons. There was a garrison of about one thousand massive fiends, armed to the teeth and clad in armor, ready to attack a city where thousands of innocent creatures lived. Our friends and teammates, our family was there.

Harper was right. There was no other way to stop the daemons from attacking Azure Heights. We had to reveal ourselves and convince them that *we'd* come to *them*, so they wouldn't go looking for us…

29

HARPER

(DAUGHTER OF HAZEL & TEJUS)

"How do we do this?" Caia whispered.

"I think we should split into three teams," Jax replied. "Caia, you can cover Blaze's back as you sneak up the tower. Stay hidden. Harper will work with Lord Kifo, and I'll take Hansa. We'll reveal ourselves to the garrison, make some noise and have them chase us around the square. But you'll have to move fast. They'll be coming for us."

I looked around, trying to find the nearest exit point. Using my True Sight, I scanned the entire area on a one-mile radius and figured we had plenty of side streets and tall, black stone walls and fences to hide behind, while Blaze went all fire and fury on the daemons in the square.

My gaze was drawn to King Shaytan, who was occasionally glancing in our direction, a smirk tugging at the corner of his mouth. I didn't think anything of it—we were wearing the original invisibility spell, with no air ripples, nothing.

He continued to tell his subjects and soldiers about how great their daemon nation was and all that other clichéd propaganda that I'd read and heard from numerous other megalomaniacs during Earthly history classes.

They were all the same to me. Evil and determined to do nothing but harm, yet charismatic and influential enough to move an entire nation to do horrible things on their behalf. The Imen had suffered long enough because of these monsters. Over the past couple of years, so had the Exiled Maras. It was time to bring it all to a grinding halt.

I was scared. I was downright terrified of what came next. There were too many of them, but we had to do something. We couldn't let them spill onto the surface. They seemed too thirsty, too eager to draw innocent blood.

"How do we do this, then?" I breathed.

"Dirt, blood, whatever's handy. We smear ourselves and make some noise," Hansa replied.

"I honestly cannot wait to take a shower already," I muttered, then froze.

King Shaytan was looking in our direction again, but there was something strange about his expression. He wasn't just glancing our way. His eyes were fixed on mine. My heart stopped for a split second as I checked my arms—I was still perfectly invisible. *So what the...*

"Wait," I whispered, looking at Shaytan.

He was grinning. His white teeth were out, his canines protruding as sharp fangs. He was holding his staff in front of him, his eyes glimmering behind the layer of red garnet, and he was watching *me*. Literally. Watching. Me.

Time stopped altogether. All the noises around me disappeared as the realization crashed into me. Weightlessness took over before dread turned my feet into blocks of lead. *Oh, no... He can see us.* I opened my mouth, but no sound came out. My voice failed me.

"I see you," King Shaytan said, looking right at us.

"He can see us," I managed.

He could see us through the red garnet.

30

FIONA

(DAUGHTER OF BENEDICT & YELENA)

The White Star Hotel was even more beautiful in the evening. Vincent had arranged for our dinner table to be set in a gorgeous glass enclosure, an extension to the grand dining room. We could see the night sky above, clearing as it unveiled billions of stars and all three moons rising. The hotel was surrounded by a beautiful garden, a plethora of trees and colorful flowers displayed between low-hedged greenery lines that formed a majestic maze.

The glass enclosure itself was stylishly decorated, with crystal chandeliers glimmering overhead and white floral arrangements to match the pristine white porcelain dinnerware and silk napkins. We were treated to a fine selection of blood mixtures, with various spices and exotic flavors.

"I guess this is what you call a 'fine dining experience'," I muttered as I sipped a particularly spicy blend from a crystal flute glass, the stem delicately engraved with gold filigree.

A lonely set of strings played somewhere in the background, at the hands of a young Iman musician. Waiters kept their distance, standing by the archway leading back into the dining room in order to give us some privacy.

My mind kept wandering back to Zane and his peculiar attachment to me, while Vincent talked about plans for the city's future. They'd been discussing a mass exodus for a couple of days, but the Lords weren't ready to really consider it as an option. If anything, Darius's death had provided even more determination for the Exiled Maras to push back against the rising threat of daemons.

"Like I said before, we could both do with some pampering after the past couple of days." Vincent gave me a gentle smile as he drank his blood.

"Yes, well, life isn't meant to be boring anyway," I replied, my gaze drifting through the glass enclosure, while Vincent's eyes were fixed on me. He seemed to want more from me, romantically speaking, but I couldn't reciprocate. I liked him, but there was no spark, nothing to make me hold my breath whenever he came near me.

You mean, like when Zane pressed you up against the wall and breathed in your scent?

I shook my head and took a deep breath, rattled by my own treacherous conscience. *What the hell am I thinking?*

"My life hasn't been the same since you came to this world,"

Vincent said, his gaze softening as I looked at him. Warmth spread through my cheeks, and I felt slightly uncomfortable. I wasn't good at letting people down in an easy, non-hurtful way. Not that diplomacy was a weak point of mine, but I'd always found the bare truth to be more... effective.

In this case, however, Vincent was already dealing with enough—a city under siege by soul-eating daemons, his sister running off to live with one such daemon, and two of his elders killed just the night before. Two uncles of his, Rowan's cousins, had perished in the explosions. He had enough on his plate, and I could tell, from the occasional flickers of sadness in his eyes, he wasn't going to feel any better if I flat-out turned him down.

"Thank you, Vincent." I nodded slowly, then decided it was time to change the subject. "So, tell me, why doesn't your library hold any literature or archives on Imen culture? I noticed that the other day, when I was doing research for our mission. There's absolutely nothing from their lore in that massive place..."

"Nice deflection," he laughed lightly, "but I'll humor you nonetheless. We don't keep any Imen culture because we... well, we sort of keep our civilizations separate."

"How so? You're sharing a city, after all."

"True, but we founded this city. We designed every building. We built it and helped it thrive. The Imen simply chose to live here with us, rather than with their own beyond the gorges. There were rules in place, and preserving our Mara heritage was a prerequisite. I hear they keep some of their own books and stories in little shops, somewhere on the lower levels, but I never bothered to read any of their folklore tales. The library is ours. I'd be more than happy to suggest a couple of decent Imen bookshops you could check out, if you'd like?"

"Sounds reasonable," I murmured, though not really impressed with this... elitist separation. It was as if the Imen weren't "good enough" to be included in the library, but they were "good enough" to work the reception desk.

"To be honest, most of the Imen who stayed with us didn't know how to read or write." Vincent shrugged. "The ones who did kept mostly to themselves and passed the skill down from one generation to another, but they never bothered to... say, open a school and educate the others. In fact, I think you care more about the Imen's culture than the Imen themselves."

Looking at it from that perspective, I couldn't help but agree with Vincent's point. This city was becoming more complex with each day that went by. Its varied nuances seemed downright contradictory at times, but the overall image was pretty clear: on one hand, we had the stylish, elitist, and art-loving Maras who considered themselves noble and superior, and, on the other hand, we had the Imen—the "simpletons", the servants and helpers, the second-class citizens. And somehow, they lived together in apparent harmony, threatened only by daemons.

But then came the whole mind-bending issue, like a big

black stain that destroyed the picture, turning the Maras into secretive creatures I couldn't trust at all. Not even Vincent...

We couldn't exactly point fingers at them, either. The situation was already difficult and complicated enough. Sparking a diplomacy war over their treatment of Imen wasn't in our best interest—yet. Once we managed to reach out to Calliope, however, we *were* going to address the issue. Until then, all I could do was be quiet and observe everything related to the mind-bending of Imen.

"But enough about them." Vincent sighed, then stood and offered me his hand. "Shall we dance?"

He winked at the musician, who switched to a deep but beautiful ballad. Its melody was soft and relatively linear, but the higher notes made my lips stretch into a smile, and I joined him on the white marble dancefloor for a dance.

Vincent held me close, one hand resting on my hip, as we swayed to the music. He studied me intently, with a mixture of curiosity and adoration, his citrus scent tickling my senses. I placed my left hand on his shoulder, my fingertips enjoying the velvety feel of his dark green jacket. He was, by all means, an elegant Mara with a keen sense of fashion. I realized then that I could never fall in love with someone like him. My peculiar strength made me yearn for someone who could handle it— and me, a warrior of sorts...

I glanced around the glass enclosure again, my eyes wandering aimlessly as the song carried us through its steady rhythm. My eyes nearly popped out at the sight of Zane standing outside, watching us. My grip on Vincent's shoulder instinctively tightened as I stared at the daemon—the look on his face was a mixture of irritation and amusement. Had he never seen people dancing before? Or did he have an issue with my dancing with Vincent, in particular?

Also, what the hell is he doing here?

"Ouch!" Vincent broke me out of my shock. "Fiona, ouch…"

I stilled, realizing I'd been squeezing his shoulder *hard*. A gasp left my throat, and I immediately took my hand back.

"I am so sorry," I mumbled, covering my mouth with both hands. He chuckled, then resumed the dancing pose, reclaiming control over my hip and right arm.

"It's okay," he said, and spun me around.

I briefly scanned the garden outside, but I couldn't see Zane anymore. Had I imagined him there? If so, why?

"The sky is beautiful tonight." I sighed, looking up. A sea of twinkling stars stretched overhead, against an indigo backdrop. Vincent, however, was unable to take his eyes off me.

"It pales in comparison to you," he breathed, gradually lowering his head in an attempt to bring his lips closer to mine.

Oh, crap, he's going to kiss me. No, no… Not a good idea…

I caught movement in the corner of my eye. Zane was once again standing on the other side of the glass, staring at us with discontent. My cheeks caught fire. My blood was simmering.

What the hell is his problem?

"What the…" I muttered, downright irritated.

"Are you okay, Fiona?" Vincent's question broke my train of

thought. I blinked a few times, then shifted my focus back to him and smiled.

"Yes... Sorry, I'm a bit tired. My mind keeps running off in different directions," I replied, then checked the garden again. Zane was gone. Again. I was starting to oscillate between the potential loss of my sanity and the possibility that the daemon was actually trying to mess with my head.

He wasn't there to physically hurt me; otherwise he would've done so. With or without the yellow powder, Zane seemed more than capable of knocking me off my feet, and even killing me. I needed more time to learn his fight patterns if I wanted to survive a potential attack from him. He was too damn fast, to begin with.

I saw him again, on the west side this time. *He's doing this on purpose.*

Not willing to give him the satisfaction of disrupting my dinner and dance with Vincent, I decided to ignore him.

"How is Rewa holding up?" I asked, wrapping my arms around Vincent's neck, in an attempt to show Zane that he wasn't going to win this.

"She's... She's fine, for the most part. It will take some time for her to... heal." Vincent blinked several times, both confused and excited by my gesture. I didn't even realize how he might interpret this—I'd been too focused on sticking it to Zane. He put his arms around my waist and pulled me closer to him, as we kept dancing.

He felt nice and warm. But the closeness didn't make my heart flutter.

"Do you think she'll pull through as Lady of Azure Heights?" I replied.

"I know she'll do her best to live up to her father's expectations," he muttered, his gaze darkening as he inched closer, his lips almost touching mine.

I pulled my head back slowly, prompting him to frown slightly, and saw Zane again—this time much closer, still on the west side of the glass enclosure.

"That's it." I exhaled sharply and gently pushed myself away from Vincent's arms.

He looked confused, almost upset.

"Did I do something to offend you?" he asked, and I genuinely felt sorry for him.

"No, not at all, Vincent. It's my fault." I shook my head, trying to control my frayed nerves as my gaze darted between him and Zane, who was blatantly standing several feet away in the garden, arms crossed over his chest, looking as if he'd just eaten a whole, raw lemon. "I'm tired and unable to focus... I think it's time I go get some rest. Please, rest assured, you've been a wonderful host. Thank you for dinner and the company..."

A couple of seconds went by as Vincent processed my excuse, then sighed and put on a half-smile.

"I understand," he said. "Shall I walk you to the inn?"

"No!" I replied, a little too loudly. *Try to soften it a bit...* "No, don't worry, I'll be fine. I can take care of myself, remember?"

I gave him a playful smirk, as I felt him drifting into a sad state that I didn't want to feel responsible for. He slipped his hands into his pockets, then stepped forward and dropped a kiss on my cheek. His lips were soft and warm. Zane was still there, carved in dark stone as he glared at me.

What is his problem?!

"Thank you for joining me for dinner tonight, Fiona," Vincent whispered.

"Have a good night, Vincent," I said, then waved goodbye and walked away, passing through the dining room filled with elegant Maras enjoying their blood dinners in the warmth of candle lights.

Never had a flame burned as hot as I did in that instant. Zane was playing a very dangerous game with me. And I wasn't going to let him win.

He might be bigger and stronger than me, but he is not going to mess with my head anymore! Not while I still have something to say about it!

31

FIONA

(DAUGHTER OF BENEDICT & YELENA)

After I got out of the hotel, I went on a quick tour of the property, including the lavish gardens outside the glass hall, looking for Zane, but there was no sign of him. That just made me angrier. I was looking forward to giving him a piece of my mind, after he'd just sabotaged my whole evening.

It wasn't about the dinner and dance part, really. I would've been fine without that. But I needed Vincent in a relaxed state if I wanted to fish for information about the Imen and the Maras' treatment of them. It was meant to be a gradual thing—from a casual dinner and conversation to, hopefully, getting more insights on the Imen's lives in Azure City. Given that we were doing our best to avoid a diplomatic crisis while helping the Maras against the daemon threat, I had to tread carefully, and Zane's interference was downright sabotage.

I cursed under my breath and proceeded to walk back to the Broken Bow Inn and call it a night. My feet hurt, as I wasn't used to wearing heels, but I could hold my own until I reached my room. The streets were relatively quiet, since it was past midnight. Several Maras were still out, along with Imen leaving the taverns and heading back to their homes—some were rowdy patrons, but most were servants and chambermaids coming from their evening shifts.

I reached the third floor with a feeling that I was being watched. I glanced over my shoulder, but I couldn't see anything. The midnight winds started rising, bringing a chill to my bones. The memory of my encounter with Zane back at Lemuel's bookstore kept replaying in my head. It was becoming increasingly difficult to get his scent off my mind.

"You look ravishing in that dress." Zane's voice startled me.

His presence suddenly weighed on me, and I turned around and faced him. My anger returned in waves of hot and cold, filling me up with the energy I needed to confront him. I scowled at him, though I had to crane my neck back in order to look him in the eyes. His red gaze burned through me.

"What the hell were you thinking back there?" I poked him in the chest with my finger. It seemed to amuse him, as his lips stretched into a lascivious smile. "What is it that you want from me? Why are you stalking me?"

Zane shrugged, giving me an innocent look. My palms were itching, and I wondered if I could slap him and get away with it.

"I'm not sure yet," he replied, his eyes narrowing as he

scanned my face for a reaction, "but I am interested in you. At least until I figure out what to do with you. You are still quite an enigma, but I'm sure I'll get my answers soon."

"Can you be a little bit more specific?" I sighed, rolling my eyes. "I've already told you what I am, what I can do, and where I'm from. In fact, you have seen some of my skills in action, if I'm not mistaken."

"You know what? I'm not really interested in talking about it... at least not right now," he said. "How about I walk you home instead?"

"I don't have a home here. What I do have is a room at the inn down below," I retorted, feeling irritated. My temperature spiked. "But there is absolutely no need for you to accompany me there. I am perfectly capable of walking back to my room without any assistance. Especially from you."

"Are you sure?" He raised an eyebrow at me, making me doubt my own decision. *What are you thinking? Of course you can walk back on your own!* "These are dangerous streets, you know..."

I kept walking, turning my back on him. "It feels pretty safe for me around these parts, since we set up that protection spell and—"

I came to a halt, my muscles suddenly clenching as I broke into a cold sweat, realizing something that I should have noticed since my encounter with Zane at the bookstore. The protection spell did not work at all. Even with all the modifications, Patrik's spell did not keep the daemons out of Azure Heights. Zane was living proof.

"Oh no..." I gasped, slowly turning around to face my devilishly handsome nightmare. "Oh no, no, no! You have got to be kidding me..."

His eyes flared red, watching quietly as I struggled to cope with the reality that the city was still open to daemon attacks. With everything that had been going on, it wasn't exactly surprising that I had lost track of this one tiny but extremely important detail. It wasn't like I could just summon a daemon to test the protective spell...

"Took you long enough." Zane smirked.

I could have slapped myself. I should've realized this sooner.

"Why didn't I see this? Why didn't I notice it earlier?" I mumbled, walking away in a daze. I nearly flew down the stairs, the urgency hitting me hard, like ice water against my bare skin. "I should have seen this..."

I needed to tell Patrik. It meant that we had to be extra vigilant once more. *And there goes my sleep for the night...*

Zane decided to accompany me anyway, walking by my side as I rushed toward the second level. I felt his eyes on me but refused to look at him. I was way too angry—at myself, but also at him.

"So what's going on between you and the redhead?" he asked. Assuming he meant Vincent but not willing to play into this scheme, whatever it was, I shrugged and decided to play the ingénue instead.

"Whatever do you mean?"

"Vincent. Of House Roho," he replied bluntly, adding weight to each word. "Is he courting you?"

Aha! So he does know more than he is letting on!

"Do you know him? You know the other Maras, too? How much do you know about this city?" I shot back, my fists so tight that my nails were digging into my skin. I looked at him, and he averted his gaze and focused on a distant point ahead. Something told me I'd hit a soft spot.

"No, I just have very good hearing," he muttered. "You mentioned his name more than once during dinner. Which, by the way, smelled quite nice from outside, though I kind of feel sorry for your species. You don't eat souls, you can't eat meat... It just feels drab, if all you get to enjoy is blood."

I scoffed once more, and kept walking, increasing my speed in order to get away from him. He wasn't being helpful, yet he was asking a lot of questions. I had to tip the scales a little bit. He kept up with me as we reached the bottom of the stairs. The Broken Bow Inn was just a few minutes away, farther down.

"You seem upset," Zane said.

"I just don't understand why you're so interested in me and my relationship to the people around me," I replied.

"I am simply making assessments as to whether you are worth saving or not, ahead of what is coming."

I stopped walking again, and turned to look at him once more. It was becoming increasingly frustrating to try to get any information out of Zane. He was so cryptic and unwilling to tell me anything that could be of use to us, and yet he could not stay away. Meanwhile, an ominous feeling crept up my spine. I knew for a fact that what he *wasn't* telling me made the difference between us walking out of this alive and us getting carried out, feet forward.

"You love talking in riddles, don't you?" I muttered, my hand slipping into a secret pocket that I had cut into my dress. I'd slipped a knife in there earlier, for just such an occasion. He gave me a half-smile and inched closer, enough for the air between us to get thicker and heavier.

"I just don't like giving away all my secrets at once," he breathed.

With one swift move, I brought my blade up to his throat, the sharp metal digging into his tan skin. He stilled, slowly raising his hands in a defensive gesture. A grin slit his face, but it was all he could do.

"Oh my, well done," Zane said. "Impressive speed. You're learning fast..."

"Tell me the truth, unless you want me to slit your throat and let you bleed to death right here," I hissed, menacingly baring my fangs. Judging by the glimmer in his eyes, he seemed to like that, which immediately made me press my lips together in a thin line. I couldn't give him any sort of satisfaction.

A couple of moments went by in sinister silence. I wondered if my knife against his throat might make him talk. He didn't seem bothered. If anything, he was amused. That just riled me up even more.

Something hit the cobblestone behind me with a sharp noise. I instinctively glanced over my shoulder, just to make sure that I wasn't going to get attacked by someone else—especially not another daemon.

It was all Zane needed to blow more yellow powder in my face as soon as I turned my head.

Damn it, how many more times am I going to fall for this?

"Crap, not again..." I wheezed and coughed, and everything went dark.

32

HERON

After our talk with Lemuel, we went back to the Broken Bow Inn, just as the third moon reached its highest point in the starry night sky. I dropped Avril off at her room and slipped into the shower in my own. I welcomed the cold water against my skin—I could make sense of almost everything that had happened to us over the past couple of days, but the one thing I had yet to wrap my head around was how I felt about Avril.

Restlessness took over, and I put on a pair of pants and started pacing the room. Something had developed between us, something very intense. It heated me up whenever Avril was near me. I had an urge to see her again, even though it had only been twenty minutes since we'd last spoken. Literally.

I had already been attracted to her long before Neraka, but the dynamic between us had changed—particularly since our accidental Pyrope back in the gorges. To say that I was conflicted was a serious understatement. I wanted to talk to her. I *needed* to be near her. There was something about Avril that made me think I had a chance at a soulmate after all.

At the same time, I was afraid of another rejection, since I had really messed it up the last time. I sure as hell wasn't looking to get slapped, or worse, again. What made things even worse, for me at least, was my near certainty that Avril felt the same way. My body and my soul were battling it out with my brain, and I had very little faith in the latter. My instincts had kept me alive for years in Azazel's prison. Why was my brain interfering?

Probably because Avril isn't just any other female; probably because she is the best thing that has ever happened to you, and you have no idea what to do with that.

I exhaled sharply and scraped away at the bottom of my heart, until I found the courage I needed to go to her room and tell her how I felt. Given the mess we were in, and the possibility that our lives might come to an abrupt end, it made no sense to hide my feelings any longer.

Who knew what tomorrow would bring?

I found myself standing outside her door. My palms were sweaty, my pulse was racing, and my stomach was starting to bother me—as if thousands of needles had filled it. It hurt like hell. As much as I racked my brain for something intelligent to say to her, I couldn't think of anything.

She was by far the most beautiful and fierce creature I had

ever come across. As much as I wanted her, and as much as some might have said I deserved it, my previous philandering made me feel unworthy of her attention.

Get it together, man...

I cursed under my breath. I had been brave enough to make it to her door, and yet I seemed to have no strength left to freakin' knock.

After a couple of deep breaths, I raised my hand, and just as my knuckles were about to touch the door, it opened. Avril stood before me, freshly showered and changed into a training suit, her hair wet and her skin smelling of roses and lavender. She looked surprised to see me, while all I could do was stare blankly at her.

The effect she had on me was close to devastating, and all I wanted was to lose myself in her, in everything she was, and in everything we could be together. I was in so much trouble.

33

AVRIL

(DAUGHTER OF LUCAS & MARION)

For some reason, Heron was standing outside my door. The look on his face startled me, because it was exactly what I had seen of myself just minutes earlier, in the mirror. My temperature spiked, as I wasn't sure why he was there in the first place.

I had been meaning to talk to him about Pyrope, about what it meant to him. I couldn't find the right words, mainly because I knew how important it was to him, as opposed to how it had taken place. We had obviously not planned for it, but it was still a very intimate gesture—especially between the two of us. I was clearly into Heron, and maybe him being here was a sign that I should talk to him about it. It had been eating away at me since yesterday.

We stared at each other, quiet and blank, as I tried and

failed miserably to formulate a coherent sentence. I had opened the door to go talk to him, and yet here he was, somehow one step ahead of me. Unless he wasn't here to talk about us. In which case, my internal turmoil was pretty much useless.

"Hey..." he muttered, a glimmer of fear lingering in his jade eyes. "I was wondering... I can't sleep... Do you think we could just hang out for a little while longer?"

I blinked several times, registering what he had just said. My brain was moving in slow motion. I was supposed to say something, but all I could do was open my mouth—no words came out.

"Sorry to intrude, but I just didn't feel like being on my own in that room." He scratched the back of his neck, then followed it up with a shrug, like a little boy who couldn't think of a better excuse. In many ways, Heron was exactly that. And the funniest thing was that it was definitely one of the reasons I liked him so much.

"It's okay," I murmured. "I was just about to come check up on you anyway, for pretty much the same reason... I don't want to be alone either. Not after everything that has happened..."

I stepped aside, allowing him to come in. Fire poured hotly through my veins. It had become a common symptom whenever he was around—my blood simmering, my head feeling light, and my stomach tightening, all signals from my body letting me know that I was definitely and irrevocably into him.

He walked across the room, then stopped by the window and turned to face me. He shoved his hands in his pockets, his gaze wandering around for about half a minute before it settled on my face.

"Yesterday was crazy, right?" I managed, already mentally slapping myself. There were plenty of better conversation openers than that.

Heron gave me a half-smile as he leaned against the window frame. He had this way of looking so deep into my eyes that it felt as though he were reaching into my very soul.

"You could say that." He nodded slowly. "But you'll have to be more specific, because there has been a lot of crazy going on since we got here. We might not be thinking about the same thing..."

"Well, what were *you* thinking about?" I replied, trying to get my senses in my body under control.

His gaze softened, and he crossed his arms over his chest. Maybe a minute went by before he spoke, but he didn't give me an answer. Something told me he was just as nervous as me, if not more so. We had gotten off to a rocky start, and we had mutually agreed that friendship was our best move forward. And yet, we were standing in front of each other, fidgeting, as an invisible magnetic force pulled us closer together.

"Is it okay if I spend the night here?" he asked.

I was speechless. What did he mean? Was he being literal? *Why the hell am I not asking him that?*

"What... Um, what do you mean?" I mumbled.

"Like, sleep. In this room. With you," he replied, then immediately corrected himself. "I mean, not in the same bed with you. I'm not... I wouldn't... It's not what I was implying... I can sleep on the sofa."

He pointed at the divan positioned at the foot of the bed. It was rather small for Heron, but not impossible for him to actually sleep in. The question was... did I want to sleep in the same room with Heron? Well, I didn't want him to go...

"Um, yeah, if you want to." I shrugged, trying not to make a big deal out of it, even though alarm bells were already ringing in my head—not because of him, but because of how happy I was about this sleepover.

He nodded, then lay on the sofa, his long legs stretching well beyond the armrest. Nevertheless, he seemed determined to make it work. I grabbed a blanket from the bottom of the dresser and handed it over to him. Our fingers touched, and thousands of electrical currents buzzed through me. It was both scary and exhilarating at the same time.

I blew out the candles on the wall sconces, then hid beneath the soft and heavy bedcover, letting the silence fall between us once more. I looked at the shuttered window, going over the events of the day in an attempt to stop myself from listening to his heartbeat. It was rapid, restless, and told me so much more than his words. It warmed me on the inside, but it also made it more difficult for me to speak up about how I felt. It was as if I knew he would respond... favorably, but I just didn't have the courage to take that step.

"What do we do tomorrow?" I asked, in the absence of

anything better to say. The air around us was charged with unspoken words.

"We can start by meeting with the rest of the team in the infirmary, first thing in the morning, like we agreed," Heron replied. I could feel his eyes on me, and if I lifted my head, I was probably going to find him looking at me, but I lacked the courage to even do that.

You coward! You were the one going after him tonight!

"Makes sense," I murmured, then stared at the ceiling, following the fine cracks in the plaster.

Minutes slipped by as I tried to find the right words to say to him. I *needed* to talk to him about how I felt. Heron needed to know that I was developing feelings for him—mainly because I wanted to understand what it could mean to him. Was he going to look at me as another conquest? Because if that was the case, I was better off chewing the bark from a tree. Or was he going to reciprocate, and rid me of my growing misery? I hated keeping things to myself, especially feelings. They always cluttered up and made me feel anxious...

"I've been meaning to talk to you," I said slowly, after a while. "About... you know, yesterday, and us. I mean, I don't really know where to start, or how to say this, but... I'm... Ah, hell, might as well spill it. I'm starting to like you, Heron. Like, really like you. Well beyond the friendzone we discussed. And I just wanted you to know that. Don't think it's an excuse for you to try to get into my pants. I'm not one of those swooning succubi you left behind back on Calliope."

There... Doesn't that feel better?

I waited for an answer, but all I got was a nearly deafening silence. My breath got stuck in my throat as I braced myself for his response – it could be literally anything and that was what scared me the most.

Then a faint grumble made it out of his chest. He was snoring...

Ugh. Way to miss the mark, Avril!

I'd bared my soul for nothing. Heron had fallen asleep already, clearly more tired than he'd seemed. The poor thing was knocked out, and I was lying here in my bed, just a couple of feet away from him, wondering if I'd be able to say those things to him again tomorrow.

My chest deflated as I sank beneath my bedcover and turned onto one side, closing my eyes. They popped back open. I was in no shape to sleep now.

This is going to be a rough night...

34

AVRIL

(DAUGHTER OF LUCAS & MARION)

I did manage to fall asleep eventually, but my dreams were not kind. Daemons surrounded me, their eyes glowing red as they clawed at my back and legs. I couldn't feel any pain, but blood poured out of me in bright red swirls, as if I were in zero gravity. My voice was muted, although I was screaming. I was kicking and punching, but they kept coming.

My nightmare only got worse, and I saw Heron beyond the sea of daemons killing me. He was running toward me, desperately reaching out and calling out my name—but I couldn't hear him either. Everything was muted. And as much as he ran, Heron wasn't getting any closer. The physics of my subconscious had rallied against me.

I gasped and opened my eyes, surrounded by quiet darkness. My sight adjusted to the obscurity, and I could make out the contours of the windows and furniture in my room. *I'm in my room... at the inn...*

Warmth enveloped me, a pair of strong arms holding me tight beneath the covers. Heat expanded through my chest as I caught his scent—a plethora of spices and musk, combined with a faint whiff of citrus from whatever soap he'd used earlier. Heron was in my bed, spooning me in a soft embrace, and I... I didn't want to be anywhere else.

"I fell off the couch a couple of times," he whispered, his hot breath tickling my ear. "I figured the bed would be more comfortable."

I didn't say anything. My words were stuck in my throat, anyway. Well, I could tell him to go back to his room if he wanted to sleep in a bed and not on my sofa, but that seemed cruel. He'd come to me for comfort and company. Besides, I was ridiculously comfortable just as I was.

His frame outweighed mine, and every curve of my body seemed to fit perfectly against his, as if someone had sculpted us as two pieces of a whole. I belonged in his arms, and every atom in me happened to agree.

What are we going to do about this? What am I going to do?

I still needed to tell him about how I felt, given my earlier failed attempt. He still needed to know that I was starting to see well beyond our physical attraction, that I was having trouble seeing him as just a friend.

I'll try again tomorrow... Maybe.

There were two ways in which this was going to go. Option

one: Heron would tell me he felt the same way, and that meant we could maybe explore this chemistry between us and see what we could make of it. That was my best-case scenario, and it still scared the hell out of me, because I'd never been in love with anyone before and I didn't understand the depths to which we could go.

Option two wasn't good. Option two had Heron telling me he wasn't interested in a serious relationship, but that we could always take advantage of our physical attraction and "have some fun". I'd heard him say that to other females back on Calliope—I knew his lines all too well. He'd tried some on me already, after all. That was my worst-case scenario, in which my feelings were one-sided and I was bound to come across as a fool, after I'd pushed him away for being a superficial philanderer.

Oh, man, I'm in for quite the ride, no matter what he says...

Of course, there was a third option, in which I could keep my mouth shut and just ignore everything between us. But who was I kidding? With every minute spent in Heron's presence, it became more and more difficult for me to just hold it in.

I'll revisit this tomorrow, with a clear, rested head.

For the time being, I figured I was better off just letting it go. Just for the night, while I was still gradually melting in his arms, while he kept me close enough for his heartbeat to echo in my chest. His breathing was even, his face hidden in my hair.

He moved in his sleep, and his lips found the back of my neck. My entire body bucked, my eyes nearly popping out of their orbits, and my skin tingled all over. He didn't do anything, but his lips settled against my neck, and that generated thousands of tiny explosions through every fiber of my body.

Oh, who the hell am I kidding?

I am falling so hard and so fast, I can't even keep up with my own body anymore...

There was plenty to love about Heron, though. Beneath his boyish charm and playful smirk, he carried years of experience, of rough living and scars of war. He was strong and determined, and downright ruthless when those he cared for were in danger. His sense of duty was out of this world—Heron knew how to obey orders but was perfectly capable of challenging them, if they interfered with his ethical code, his desire to improve the world around him.

I had a feeling that, deep down, Heron wanted to love and be loved—more than anything. It was why our unintended Pyrope had had such an impact on him. He'd thought about it. Maybe he'd even dreamed about the day he'd meet his soulmate and taste her blood on his lips.

I closed my eyes, trying to put myself back to sleep. It would take a while. His hard body against mine and his sleepy lips on my skin were making it very difficult for me to fully relax.

So I drifted for a while, simply enjoying the moment.

Simply enjoying Heron's arms around me.

35

FIONA

(DAUGHTER OF BENEDICT & YELENA)

I came to after what felt like a second. It wasn't. Zane had carried me up to my room and put me in my bed. My dress was still on, but he'd removed my shoes, as evidenced by my toes wiggling freely.

Son of a...

How did he keep fooling me with that damn yellow powder? *I need to get better at this...*

The lights were dim, and I could hear the fire crackling in the fireplace. *Oh great, he lit a fire, too. Making sure I'm comfortable in my defeat.* I groaned as I stretched my arms out, cursing under my breath and lifting my head off the pillow.

My heart jumped at the sight of Zane sitting in a chair that was too small for him. He was quiet, a dark look in his red eyes as he watched me.

"As if you couldn't get any creepier!" I spat, sitting up and scowling at him. "Now you're watching me sleep, too?"

"I was just waiting for you to wake up." He shrugged, shifting his weight in the visibly uncomfortable chair. The wood creaked as he supported part of his weight on one of the armrests. "Just being respectful here. I figured it would be rude to just plop you in here without saying a proper 'Good night!', wouldn't you agree?"

"Oh, *now* you're being respectful! After you knocked me out for... what, the fourth time? I'm losing track here!" I scoffed.

"I assumed you were into Vincent because of his manners," he replied matter-of-factly, "and probably his fashion sense, too. The latter I can do nothing about, but I can try to be a little bit more gentile. As much as I like the way you crinkle your nose when you're angry, I prefer you when you're smiling."

It took me a few seconds to register the compliment, but it didn't make me feel better. If anything, it confused me even more. What was his end game? What did he want from me?

"You could start by not blowing yellow dust in my face whenever I ask you uncomfortable questions," I shot back. "I'd classify it as more important than bidding an appropriate farewell."

"Duly noted." He nodded, then smiled. "You should get some sleep. I think you'll have a very busy day ahead of you tomorrow."

I moved to get out of bed, but stilled as I captured the hidden meaning of his words.

"What do you mean? What's happening tomorrow?" I asked, my tone flat.

"How am I supposed to know?" He raised an eyebrow, as if daring me to get all riled up.

"You just said... Ugh, never mind." I shook my head and decided to sulk, crossing my arms over my chest. "You're all cryptic and full of smoke, as usual. Completely useless."

"I wouldn't say *completely* useless." He leaned forward, his gaze drilling into me. "I still have a few tricks up my sleeve."

"You still haven't told me where you got the swamp witch magic from," I retorted, attempting a different angle. Maybe persistence could be the key to my success. Zane didn't seem like he was going anywhere, and he'd specifically admitted that he couldn't stay away. Perhaps I could use that to my advantage.

Worth a shot...

He rolled his eyes and leaned against the back of the chair, generating another round of loud creaks. I was expecting to see that thing give way under his massive frame any minute now.

"Can we, for once, not talk about such difficult topics?" He groaned, as if he were the one frustrated, not me. *The nerve!* "For once, I'd like to just sit here and look at you... to just bask in your beauty."

If it were anyone else saying such things to me, my creep-o-meter would've been screaming and flashing bright red signals. And yet, there was something in the way he spoke—maybe in his low, husky voice and smooth tone—that just put me on a different kind of edge. It made me feel extremely self-conscious, and, at the same time, it heated me up from the inside.

What was it about him that turned off my defense mechanisms and prompted my other senses to flare up? It was as if my consciousness expanded whenever he was near. He had danger written all over him, but I couldn't bring myself to treat him as a hostile force. Zane basically disarmed me, and it scared the crap out of me.

"Well, that wasn't creepy at all," I muttered.

"I'm simply being honest." He stood up, and the room seemed tiny all of a sudden. My muscles tensed as he stepped forward, closing the distance between us. He noticed my reaction, and raised his hands in a defensive gesture. "Relax, Fiona, I'm not going to hurt you or be anything but respectful toward you."

He moved closer and sat on the bed, next to me. The mattress swelled beneath me, lifting me up as he sank into it. I stared back at him as he studied my face, once more looking for my every expression, for anything that could maybe tell him what I was thinking.

"That chair was a literal pain in my ass." Zane grinned.

I almost smiled, then pressed my lips tight and looked away. I wasn't done with the sulking part.

"I really can't wrap my head around all this," I muttered. "I should kill you on sight."

"You could try." I heard the confident smile in his voice before I even saw it stretch on his face—which, by the way, looked incredibly handsome in the dim glow of the room. Dark shadows and amber strips of light played against his rugged features, bringing out his cleft chin and sharp cheekbones, and adding dramatic contours to the blade of his nose and his almond-shaped eyes. I felt a sudden urge to touch his black hair, which lay tightly braided down his back. Only then did I notice the fine gold thread woven over his horns. This was no second-class daemon I was dealing with; that much was obvious from his outfit—gold adorned the belt holding his dark brown leather loincloth over his narrow hips, and even the straps of his sandals.

"You're the enemy, Zane," I breathed.

"I'm not *your* enemy," he replied, inching closer. His gaze dropped to my lips.

"What do you want from me?"

"For the millionth time, I don't know yet," he murmured, his face barely an inch from mine. I held my breath and had no idea what to do next. My body refused to react, but my rising temperature was similar to the surface of a sun. "But I promise I will let you know as soon as I figure it out, Fiona."

"This is... strange," I managed, my heart pounding.

"The fact that I'm here? Or the fact that you're allowing me to get this close?"

"I... I don't know." My voice was barely audible, while my mind screamed at me to get a grip. "There must be something wrong with me."

"But it feels right, doesn't it?" His eyes found mine once

more, flaring red as the air between us became supercharged. I feared lightning bolts would shoot out if he came any closer.

"I... Why are you doing this?"

"Because you're not stopping me." He grinned.

A few seconds went by as we looked at each other, then time nearly stopped when Zane's lips parted. I had a feeling I knew what was coming next, and my heart was too hyped to take it. Too much was happening at once.

"Don't," I said to him, looking into his eyes.

He pulled his head back slowly, then cocked it to one side, visibly amused.

"Or what?" he replied.

"You won't like my answer."

There you are, Fiona! Where have you been? I've missed you.

"Hm. I guess I've found your limit." The shadow of a smile passed over his face. "Good to know. I love a good challenge. Now, off to bed, little vampire..."

He moved, and I instantly knew what was coming next, before he even brought a fistful of yellow powder up to my face. I slapped his hand away, the dust scattering away on the floor, and he laughed hard.

I glowered, the tension back in my muscles as I regained my senses and original anger. Zane had been planning to knock me out again.

"Like I said, you're learning fast." He gave me an appreciative nod, then stood and walked over to the window. "Get some rest, Fiona. Keep your distance from Vincent. I'll see you soon."

"Wait, what do you mean? What's your deal with Vincent? Why—" I didn't get to ask the third question. Zane had already opened the window and jumped out.

My lungs filled with the cool air. I looked outside, but there was no sign of him. Just shadows and flickering streetlamps. And a starry sky above, with three moons that seemed to have secrets of their own. That was Neraka for you—everything was hidden, even what was there in plain sight.

And Zane was the perfect example...

36

HARPER

(DAUGHTER OF HAZEL & TEJUS)

He could see us.

The king of daemons could actually see us through the red garnet of his golden staff. And he was grinning at us, not at all surprised. As if he had expected to see us here, somehow.

"Oh crap..." I breathed, my limbs suddenly soft, and my heart sinking. Caspian's hold on me tightened, as he too realized the horrific amount of trouble that we were in.

Cold water splashed us from behind, but given that we were using the original invisibility spell, it didn't do anything other than confuse the daemon that had tried to reveal us. I understood then what was happening, even though I had no way to explain how: they knew we were here. They had known we would be coming. Us being here, right up to this moment, had been part of Shaytan's plan. I could see it on his face—the tremendous satisfaction of having drawn us out.

"We need to get out of here. Now," Jax said.

The daemons created a circle around us, the crowd tightening as they drew closer, baring their fangs and claws and preparing to attack.

"Well, that's strange... What sort of spell are you using, little mice?" King Shaytan growled, keeping his eyes on us through the red garnet, then barked orders at his soldiers and the daemons surrounding us. "Use the lenses and capture them alive!"

Some of the fiends took out round, red lenses, and brought them up to their eyes to see us through them. *Oh, crap!*

They started pointing at us, sneering as the rest of the crowd got riled up, scrambling for dirt and even drawing blood from their palms to smear and reveal us—at least partially. They came at us all at once. The tighter the space around us, the harder it was going to be to get out of here in one piece.

"Split up—we'll meet at the top! Blaze, you know what to do!" Jax breathed.

Caspian pulled me after him as we darted out of the mass of daemons closing in on us. We dodged their attempts to reveal us with mud and blood, and ran as fast as we could. The fiends were spry, though, and stayed hot on our tails, as the ones with the red lenses kept shouting and pointing at us.

"The columns! They're running past the columns! There!" I heard one screech, as the crowd spilled into the streets.

All we had to do was hold on and not get caught, until Blaze could get to the top of the tower and douse them all in deadly fire. We took a sharp left turn, and the daemons tumbled down the alley after us, snarling and laughing maniacally—as if they were on a fun hunt of sorts. It sent shivers down my spine, but it also riled me up.

I shot out several pulse barriers over my shoulder, enough to knock them back a couple of feet. They *were* fast, but they had their limits, and this sentry ability of mine was one of the few effective defense mechanisms that I could rely on. It helped put a dozen more feet between us, but they kept chasing us through the city.

"This is a coordinated effort," I muttered as we turned right. "They know exactly what they're doing here!"

"We can analyze this later," Caspian cut me off, and jerked my hand.

I ran ahead, prompting him to pull me back and slip us through the crevice between two black stone buildings on the left, before the daemons turned right after us. It was his good use of that split second that got us out of their way. His quick thinking kept us hidden in that nook, while the hordes of daemons kept running forward, roaring as they searched for us.

Those red lenses must've only served to see invisible creatures directly. They didn't allow them to see through the walls—otherwise they would've captured us already.

Caspian pushed ahead through the crevice, and I held onto him until we reached the opposite end. We ended up in a narrow little alley, with tall buildings and dozens of side streets extending both left and right. We moved through the maze of black stone giants, catching glimpses of daemons, commoners, hunters, and soldiers alike, roaming through the neighboring alleys as they searched for us.

We turned left again and found a small covered terrace, bordered by a half-wall. The crowd was moving farther from our location, but it still seemed like a good idea to duck and take cover on that terrace. We had some waiting to do before Blaze got to his vantage point.

"We'll wait here for Blaze to do his thing," I murmured, pulling my knees up to my chest and supporting my back against the half-wall.

Caspian pulled me close, our hearts thundering in our chests as the gravity of what was coming next finally sank in. The fate of our team... our survival was largely in Blaze's hands. Our invisibility spell was going to wear off soon and, worst of all, it didn't fully protect us from the daemons, given those damned red lenses.

A dozen scenarios played themselves in a loop inside my head, all at once. Few led to my survival, and that made my blood freeze. Caspian's grip on my shoulders tightened.

"We'll get through this," he whispered in my ear.

The dread clawing through my stomach said otherwise.

37

HANSA

We shot through the tightening crowd toward the east side. I held onto Jax as he guided me toward a wide alley leading away from the square. We avoided spurts of blood and muddied hands—the daemons were trying to mark us, while those with red lenses kept pointing at us, directing the others after us.

We drew our swords and slashed our way out of the last dozen square feet of fiends trying to get between us and our exit, then kicked and elbowed left and right until we made it out of the crowd. Several bodies dropped behind us, causing a stampede as they all rushed after us.

Jax and I ran fast, our feet barely touching the ground. Hunters and soldiers were hot on our trail, along with those wretched red lens holders. It took several sharp turns to put some distance between us and our pursuers, but we eventually made it out of their sight when Jax pulled me into a dark alley.

There was an abandoned cart there, right next to what looked like a cellar door. I looked around the corner, seeing the daemons getting closer—the ones with lenses led the way, scanning the area. They were less than fifty yards from us, and approaching fast.

"What do we—" My voice trailed off. I watched Jax as he pulled the cart in front of the cellar door. "What are you doing?"

"Down here," Jax replied, then opened the cellar door.

Without a second thought, I jumped in, followed by Jax. He pulled it shut, and darkness enveloped us. We kept close to each other. It was a small space, with barely enough room to lie down, but it would do for the time being.

The ground above thundered, but we seemed to be safe down here. I heard the crowd of daemons rumbling nearby, but the cart that Jax had moved had successfully obscured our little escape hatch. They moved farther down the road, shouting orders to spread out and find us.

My heart was beating so fast, my lungs were having a hard time keeping up.

"How... How did this happen?" I murmured, the adrenaline still making my arms and legs shake. That had been a ridiculously close call, and we weren't even out of the woods yet. We only had a few minutes before Blaze got to the top of that tower and burned the entire area down. Only a few minutes to process what had just happened. "How did he know? How did the king know that we were there? I mean, it was a big crowd. I get that the red garnet allows him to see invisible creatures, but... how did he know we were there? Was this planned, Jax? Were we expected?"

"I don't know, Hansa, but it's clear that the daemons know more about us than we thought," he replied, his voice low and raspy as he caught his breath.

"Blaze needs to come through on this one, otherwise we're screwed..." I managed, my knees getting weak.

"We'll wait here until he does. We'll hear it," Jax said, moving closer.

He couldn't see me, but he used his hands to feel his way up my arms and over my shoulders, to find my face and cup it in his palms. My breathing was ragged and uneven, my blood broiling from what had just happened. I barely registered what he said.

"Listen, Hansa, there's a chance we won't make it out of here alive," he said gruffly, "though I'm *really* hoping it's minimal. However, I'll never forgive myself if we get killed in the next ten minutes and I don't get a chance to do this..."

His lips crashed over mine, kissing me deeply. I instantly disintegrated. He wrapped his arms around me and held me tight. My mouth welcomed him, his tongue working mine as our souls touched one another and we dissolved into a single, extremely intense being. I'd been waiting for this for so long...

Despite the madness and horror waiting for us outside, we had a handful of minutes in a cellar, and Jax had chosen to do this. To kiss me, before anything else. I could feel him—all of him. The softness of his lips, his delicious taste, and his firm grip as he deepened our kiss. He groaned as I locked my arms around his neck and pulled him even closer.

We'd finally found each other. It just so happened that we'd found each other in the underground city of murderous daemons. And there was no way in hell I was letting him go this time.

"We *are* getting out of here, Jaxxon Dorchadas," I breathed against his lips, running my fingers through his short hair. "Mark my words. I did not put up with all the uncertainty for three months, for just a peck on the lips!"

He chuckled lightly, and my whole being resonated with him. We held on tight, kissing each other's faces as we waited in the darkness of that cellar.

"I'm not letting you go, Hansa," he whispered, then covered my mouth with his and took me on another ride through the stars.

Sure, there were daemons outside looking for us. But we had a little time to communicate everything we'd kept from each other—every touch, every kiss, and every sigh was an unspoken declaration of love. Neither of us was good at putting our emotions into words, but damn, his lips knew how to get the message across...

38

CAIA

(DAUGHTER OF GRACE & LAWRENCE)

E verything happened incredibly fast from the moment Blaze squeezed my hand and guided us through the crowd. Our objective was the palace tower, but we were surrounded by bloodthirsty daemons who wanted us captured.

We both ran as fast as we could, steering clear of fiends lunging at us, dodging others who shouted as we moved forward, struggling to make our way to the palace stairs.

My heart viciously thudded in my chest as I flipped one of my lighters out. I caught a glimpse of a red lens to my right, accompanied by a snarl and followed by a spray of blood.

Damn it!

They'd managed to mark me, and it made me a visible target. My thumb pressed the lighter button, and I channeled a fraction of my focus into generating a defensive fire to help put some distance between us and the daemons.

Sparks came out and grew into a blazing sphere, but I never got to let it loose. The horde behind us was horrifyingly fast, and one of them slapped my hand. My lighter got lost in the scuffle.

All of a sudden, just as we dashed forward, the crowd moved back. Before I had a chance to realize what was going on, a thick cloud of yellow dust swallowed us.

Oh no...

I coughed and wheezed, but kept running for maybe a couple more seconds, before everything went dark.

"Blaze!" I cried out.

I heard him grunt just as my body turned to what felt like liquid. Losing control over my senses was the gateway to despair. Fear poured cold through my veins, and my throat closed up. I hit the stone pavement.

The daemons growled and cheered my fall. I couldn't see anything, and, bit by bit, I started to shut down. My mouth opened, but I couldn't hear myself speak. Soon enough, I couldn't hear anything anymore...

I was lost in the darkness, in a sea of daemons, and all I could think of was...

What of the others?

39

HARPER

(DAUGHTER OF HAZEL & TEJUS)

At least ten minutes went by. We sat there, hidden behind the half-wall of a terrace, lost in a maze of narrow streets, waiting to hear a dragon roaring and thousands of daemons screaming as they burned to a crisp in the city square. But those sounds never came.

"Something's wrong," I whispered, my entire body trembling. "Where's Blaze? Why hasn't he transformed yet?"

Caspian didn't answer, but I felt his fingers digging into my shoulder. It was too late, though. For the first time in my life, I was experiencing real panic. Shortness of breath, a rapid heartbeat, and a dizzying succession of hot and cold waves crashed into me as I began to fear the worst.

"What if they got to them?" I gasped, then used my True

Sight to look around, until I found the city square, east of our position. "Oh, no..."

"What?" Caspian's voice echoed somewhere in the back of my head as I fell to my knees.

They'd caught them. Daemons had gathered back in the square, two bodies being carried up the stairs toward King Shaytan. They'd been covered in dirt and blood, and they were unconscious—Caia and Blaze, from their now-visible general features.

My heart sank and broke into thousands of little pieces. I gripped the edge of the half-wall so tight that pieces of it crumbled beneath my fingers.

"Harper," Caspian said, "what do you see?"

"They... They got them," I cried out, no longer able to hold it together. My eyes burned with tears, but I kept watching. The daemons tied Caia and Blaze with rope, and carried them inside the palace. King Shaytan gave more orders, his soldiers once again spreading out. They were going to look for us, probably turn the entire city upside down if they had to. "They got Blaze and Caia..."

Several seconds went by. Caspian's arms came around me, pulling me close to his chest. I caved in, crying uncontrollably as my mind came to terms with what I'd just witnessed. I wanted to scream and go after them, but I also knew I didn't stand a chance at this point. The rest of my team and an entire city of innocent Maras and Imen relied on me.

"Harper." His voice was low and comforting as he held me

tight, his lips moving against the top of my head. "Shaytan's not going to kill them. You heard him. He wants them alive. He probably wants information before he does anything else with them..."

"Anything else?" I managed, sniffing and wiping at the stream of tears pouring out of my eyes.

"Don't think about that for now," he replied gently. "They've got time. Which means we've got time to make this right. They know we're here, so chances are they won't go into the city tonight. Let's just focus on what we have to do next. The city is under a protection spell, anyway, so if daemons do go there tonight, they won't be able to do anything."

I sobbed against his chest for another minute, before my logic stepped in. It wasn't in my nature to get emotional, and, as it turned out, my body had a defense mechanism against a potential complete meltdown.

"Okay," I sighed, working my way back to my good old self, "we need to focus... I... We need to prioritize."

"What are you thinking?" Caspian asked. His support and patience had not gone unnoticed. I knew I would reward him for his incredible support at some point. He held me up in ways I'd never even imagined until five minutes earlier.

"We need to find Hansa and Jax, ideally," I replied, then gave the palace another glance with my True Sight. Caia and Blaze had been carried inside, but I couldn't see where, exactly. Whether it was the distance or some invisibility spell at work, I wasn't sure yet. But at least I knew where they were keeping my friends. I knew where to go. "We need a safe spot to work out a plan, and get Blaze and Caia out of there."

"Shaytan will probably have a way of containing the dragon," Caspian said.

"We'll cross that bridge when we get to it." I shook my head. "You've been in this city before. Where is it safe for us to be, at least for a couple of hours?"

"Mose's hut is a good bet," he murmured. "Nobody will think to look for us there because nobody knows about our connection to Mose. It's also close to the safest route out of the city, so we might see Hansa and Jax around there, if we can't find them in this area."

As my head cleared, more questions popped up. The most burning one rolled off my tongue.

"Did they follow us all the way from the city? Did they know we were coming, Lord Kifo?"

"I wouldn't exclude the possibility," he muttered. Anger vibrated in his voice.

"GASP was betrayed, then... somehow..." I sighed, then rubbed my face. "Ugh! I don't get it! Was the whole army parade from earlier just for show? Did he already know we'd be here? How... How did it get to this?"

"I don't know, but we'll get out of here. All of us."

I wished I could see his face as he spoke those words of encouragement. I wanted to see his resolve, and draw strength from it. I couldn't suspect Caspian of anything at this point—

not anymore, as he was stuck with me, struggling by my side, while thousands of daemons lurked around, looking for us.

"I'll get them out," I whispered, as he held me tight.

"I have no doubt that you will, Harper..."

Hearing him call me by my first name felt strangely comforting. His encouragement coaxed my mind into overdrive, and I gathered the resolve I needed to stand up, taking his hand in mine.

"Let's go to Mose's hut," I said, my heart filled with determination and anger. "We've got a dragon and a fae to rescue."

And that was just at the top of my list, I realized as we snuck through the maze of stone buildings. We didn't have just Caia and Blaze to release from Shaytan's palace. We needed to find out how we'd been given away in the first place. Had someone betrayed us, or had they simply sent hunter daemons to follow us?

Our initial mission had been to gather intel—well, that had sunk to the bottom of my list of priorities, at least for the time being. Our presence here had already been given away, so, provided we managed to get Caia and Blaze out safely, we needed to get out of the daemon city and one of us would need to head back to Azure Heights to update our other team members. And then maybe we ought to head out to the western plains...

We'd been hitting our heads against a wall within the Mara city. But the Imen tribes living out in the plains could be instrumental in our investigation of everything that had been ailing

Neraka. If we couldn't get GASP to come in and help, we could try to rally the rogue Imen.

But the capture of Caia and Blaze had hit a soft spot in me, and it was all I could focus on in this moment. I'd already nearly lost Fiona to these fiends; I sure as heck wasn't going to let them have our dragon and fire fae.

40

BLAZE

E verything had happened so fast. One minute, I'd grabbed
Caia's hand, and we were running. The next, a puff of
yellow dust and darkness.

*My eyes peeled open, and saw nothing but metal
surrounding me.*

What the...

Caia!

I sat up with a groan, my head hurting. Sharp pain stabbed
right through my brain as I tried to make sense of my environment. I breathed a sigh of relief when I saw Caia lying next to
me, slowly coming to.

My pulse started racing as I understood exactly where we
were. They'd captured us. Then, they'd crammed us into a
metallic box of sorts. Caia's moan caught my attention.

"Are you okay?" I asked, brushing her hair back with my fingers so I could see her face. She seemed all right, just mildly dazed as she looked up at me.

"What... What happened?" she managed.

"They got us," I replied, then helped her up.

The box was just one head taller than me in a standing position, and several feet wide—enough for me to lie down, but not much else. The air felt heavy, my chest tightening as mild claustrophobia set in. I wasn't used to such small spaces, and I knew I couldn't stay in here for too long. My inner dragon was already roaring, begging for release.

"Blaze... the yellow powder," she gasped, remembering our attempt to escape the crowd and get to the tower. "It's the same as what Zane used on Fiona... Son of a... We were 'Zaned'!"

She was getting angry. I placed my hands on her shoulders, needing her calm and composed.

"Caia, deep breaths," I said softly. "We *have* to keep cool..."

She nodded slowly, then frowned as she looked around. "What is this place?"

"I don't know." I knocked on the metal wall, listening to the hollow clang. "But this is meranium."

"So, daemons can't get to us and eat our souls?" She seemed confused, and I couldn't blame her. This didn't make much sense to me either. What did make sense was the dire set of circumstances in which we'd found ourselves, as my limited options became clear.

"The answer to your question would be yes. This little box

will stop daemons from eating our souls." I sighed, then punched the wall to test its hardness. My knuckles hurt, and the metal did not bend. "And it looks like it will stop me from going dragon, too."

"Wait, what?" She blinked a few times, horror draining the color from her face. "You... You can't?"

"I could try." I scratched the back of my neck. "But I might end up killing you in the process before I manage to break the box... I still have my fire breath, so I could try melting my way through one of the walls..."

"Blaze, we need to get out of here," Caia murmured. "We... We can't stay here... The others! Jax, Hansa... Harper... Lord Kifo... The city!"

"I doubt they'll go after Azure Heights with us in here." I shook my head, trying to maintain some positivity—enough to avoid despair. "I also doubt they caught the others. We're the only ones in here."

There was a loud screech beyond the wall to my right. We both stilled and stared toward it—there was a square opening at eye level, big enough for a petite creature like Caia to fit through. It extended into a long, dark tunnel, and a light shone at the end of it as someone opened the latch.

A pair of red eyes glimmered at us, and I recognized the face. King Shaytan was standing outside our meranium prison, grinning with tremendous satisfaction. My blood boiled, rage swelling my muscles. My desire to crush his skull was only outweighed by my anger at my inability to get us out of here. I'd told Caia the truth: if I were to turn into a dragon right here and now, I would crush her in the process.

And I was ready to die a thousand times, in horrific pain, before hurting a hair on her beautiful head...

"Well, someone's up early!" King Shaytan's voice boomed through the tunnel.

"What do you want from us?" I shouted, and he cackled with mocking delight.

"I already have what I want. I've got you two!"

There were at least fifty yards between us. I felt Caia's hand on my arm, squeezing gently.

"Don't let him get to you," she whispered. "He's gloating. For now, anyway. He won't be once I'm done with him..."

I was a sucker for that fire blazing inside her. Shaytan put something into the tunnel, then pushed it toward us. It rolled down, and as it got closer, I realized it was a small barrel.

"So, what, you'll keep us in here forever?" I shot back, catching the barrel as it fell out of the tunnel. I pulled the cork cap off and smelled its contents. It was filled with fresh water. I handed it over to Caia.

"I haven't decided yet." Shaytan shrugged, scratching his braided beard. "But you'll be staying in there for a while. Don't think about using any fire in there. The box is charmed, and the meranium is an exquisite conductor. You'll melt your flesh off. The walls are twenty yards thick, little dragon."

"You've really thought this through, I see," I replied, gritting my teeth.

Caia drank some of the water, then passed the barrel back to me.

"I've been watching you for a while." Shaytan smirked. "I like your... spark! Now, drink up, and get comfortable. You're not going anywhere."

He shut the latch, and darkness poured through the tunnel. I breathed heavily and looked at Caia. Her wide teal eyes trembled with anger and fear, and there wasn't much I could do about it. We only had each other, for the time being, and we were stuck in a box, deep below the surface of Neraka.

I had no idea where Harper and the others were. No way of breaking free without crushing Caia in the process...

"Blaze... what do we do?" Her voice was weak, barely audible.

It broke my heart to see her like that, especially since I didn't have anything good to tell her. All I could do was keep her close and make sure no harm would come to her. I wrapped my arms around her and held her tight, gently kissing the top of her head.

I felt her arms around my waist as she responded quietly, gradually relaxing against my body. It was all she could do, too, for the time being.

"He's not going to keep us in here forever," I said. "The others are out there, Caia. We'll get through this one way or another."

She trembled in my embrace, but I didn't let go. Caia was my source of energy, and I needed every ounce of it to prepare for what was to come.

He won't keep us here forever.

All I need is a good window of opportunity.

41

SERENA

It was well after lunch, on the second day since my sister's team had deployed for Neraka. According to our conversations via Telluris, there was definitely something strange going on there regarding all the disappearances, but they were still investigating.

Draven and I were in the Druid Archives looking through travel logs from thousands of years back, trying to find any reference to the delegation that had crash landed on Neraka. So far, unfortunately, there was nothing, but we still had about twenty volumes' worth of logs to go over.

Derek and Sofia had convened another meeting back on Mount Zur to catch up with the rest of the GASP council on the Tenebris team's progress. Apparently, the incubi insurgents were losing ground fast, and our envoy had already been effective in helping the locals drive the extremists into a corner, so to speak.

Draven was going to be briefed on talking points after the meeting, as he was determined to dig through the Druid archives first. There was something bothering him about Neraka—I could feel it, but neither of us could figure out what it was exactly.

A bell rang outside the hall, announcing the passage of another hour. Draven and I looked at each other. He gave me a brief nod, then closed his eyes. It was time to reach out to our Neraka team again.

"Telluris Harper!" he called out.

Several seconds went by, and I could see his brows furrow, though he tried to keep it from me. I found that cute, especially since our souls were in such perfect sync. I felt everything that he felt, after all.

"Telluris Harper!" he chanted again, and then his forehead smoothed. "Are you okay?"

I could tell, from the look on his face, that he'd made contact.

"What are you doing now?" he asked, then listened for a few seconds. "Is it safe? ...Okay, we'll talk again tonight. Be careful."

He sighed, then opened his eyes, his gaze settling on my face. I was on the edge of my seat, naturally worried for Harper and the others. Sure, they could handle themselves and whatnot, but I still couldn't help but be concerned.

"What's wrong?" I asked, a feeling of uneasiness taking over.

"Nothing." He shook his head. "She couldn't say much, but we'll catch up again tonight. The investigation is going ahead, and they're exploring the gorges in the Valley of Screams. She couldn't risk focusing on Telluris while down there, so we'll get a full report later tonight instead. They're all okay."

I nodded slowly, then flipped through another page of the thirteenth log I'd been studying. My gaze wandered across the page, and I bit the inside of my cheek.

"There's something you're not telling me," I muttered, unable to let go of that strange sliver of doubt that had nestled in the back of my head.

"No, it's not that, my love," Draven replied, then gave me a weak smile. "Whatever you're feeling, just get it out of your head. It's a residue of my own concerns, and, until we finish checking these logs, I can't validate any of my suspicions. There's just no point in getting worried over a hunch of mine..."

"So you do have suspicions about Neraka." I raised an eyebrow at him, then resumed reading a short line that had caught my attention a couple of seconds earlier.

"I do, yes, but nothing to warrant concern," he said, then watched me quietly. "What is it?"

There it was. The listing I'd been looking for. I moved my index finger along the line of text, recognizing the names and dates.

"I found something," I murmured. "There's a list of Druid delegations here, from the period that Rewa mentioned. There are eight of them, to be precise. But only six came back."

Draven got up and moved around the large round table, pulling up a chair to sit next to me. He checked the page as well, then scoffed as he drew an unfortunate conclusion.

"The delegation that went missing included a swamp witch, ten fae from a neighboring galaxy, seven Druids, two Maras, and twenty incubi and succubi. It was a peaceful, exploratory mission headed toward the Yaris constellation," he said, then pinched the bridge of his nose, closing his eyes for a moment.

"The Yaris constellation?" I asked, my wariness weighing heavier on my shoulders.

"It's in the direction of Neraka." He shook his head slowly. "The delegation vanished, communications completely cut off..."

"Rewa said the Exiled Maras bid the Druid delegation good-bye," I replied, my stomach churning. "Do you think it's a different delegation?"

"I doubt it," he sighed, pointing at the noted coordinates on the side. He then pulled out a map of neighboring galaxies, and showed me Neraka's cluster. "The coordinates from which the vanished delegation last communicated are eerily close to those of Neraka's galaxy. It's definitely odd."

"So, what, do you think the Exiled Maras lied? That the Druid delegation never left Neraka?"

Angst took over, and Draven instinctively took my hand in his, squeezing gently in an attempt to soothe me. He had this incredible way of immediately reacting to my emotions—and it only made me love him more.

"I'm not saying that. Not yet, anyway. I just think it warrants some investigation," he replied, inching closer, then followed it up with a reassuring smile. "I'll talk to Jax again tonight, and tell him about this, okay? He'll know what to do, since he's there."

"It seems as though the Exiled Maras were the last to see that delegation," I muttered. "He's bound to have some good questions about that, and they'd better come up with good answers..."

I crossed my arms over my chest and leaned into my chair. Draven put his arm around me, pulling me closer and dropping a flurry of short, sweet kisses on the side of my face.

"It'll be okay, Serena," he said. "They're fully grown adults, and they are more than well trained for whatever might come at them. They will reach out if they need us."

"You still feel... uneasy," I replied, resting my head in the warm place between his neck and shoulder.

"It's in my nature, my love."

While that was true—Draven wasn't the poster boy of optimism, in general—I couldn't help but wonder how much of his concern was just a manifestation of his character, and how much was worthy of special attention.

His instincts rarely betrayed him, after all. If he caught a whiff of something, it was because there was something there to begin with.

Either way, we had to wait for the evening to come so he could speak to Jax.

In the meantime, all I could do was keep my head clear and try not to worry about Harper and her team.

READY FOR THE NEXT PART OF THE SHADIANS' STORY?

Dear Shaddict,

Thank you for reading *A Den of Tricks*.

The next book in the series, ***ASOV 55: A City of Lies***, releases **January 21st, 2018.**

Lies will crumble.

Truth will unfold...

Visit www.bellaforrest.net to order your copy.

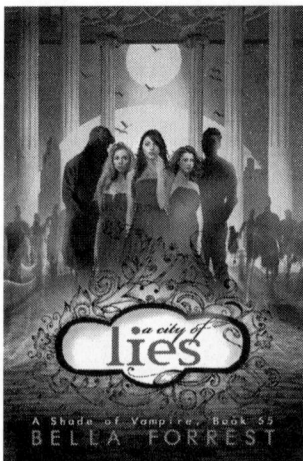

I'll see you there!

Love,

Bella x

P.S. Join my VIP email list and I'll send you a personal reminder as soon as I have a new book out. Visit here to sign up: **www.forrestbooks.com**

(Your email will be kept 100% private and you can unsubscribe at any time.)

P.P.S. Follow The Shade on Instagram and check out some of the beautiful graphics: @ashadeofvampire

You can also come say hi on Facebook: www.facebook.com/AShadeOfVampire

And Twitter: @ashadeofvampire

Made in the USA
Lexington, KY
08 January 2018